Gold, Greed, and Good Dogs

Oh...and a fish!

And a watch.

Don't forget the watch!

An Alphonse "Dave" Davecki *Cold* Case

Savage PRESS

Betsy Bowen drawing

Gold, Greed, and Good Dogs

Oh…and a fish!

And a watch.

Don't forget the watch!

An Alphonse "Dave" Davecki *Cold* Case

Michael Savage

First Edition

This is a work of fiction, and parody, with some feeble attempts at humor, smatterings of irony, an occasional bit of sarcasm, and the occasional flash of insight. Any resemblance to real people, places, or things is unintended or coincidental.

Reader Alert: In this and other Davecki books, sauna is a verb.

ISBN-13: 978-1-937706-25-8
Library of Congress Control Number: 2020941005

Cover Art: Amy Eliot
Additional Inside Art: Betsy Bowen
Design: Jill Johnson and Debbie Zime

Published by:
Savage Press
14172 E Carlson Rd.
Brule, WI 54880

Phone: 218-391-3070
Email: mail@savpress.com
Website: www.savpress.com

Printed in the United States of America

All the gold in Hayfield County
is in the middle of the woods
in a survivalist camp
in somebody else's name.

With a tip o' the hat to Larry Gatlin

Betsy Bowen drawing

CHAPTER 1

The frozen surface of Husky Bay provided sufficient support for walking, but the going was slow. The ice had no snow-cover. Traction was treacherous. If Jesus had been born in Iron Creek, Wisconsin, Davecki thought, walking on water would have been no big deal in the winter. The black and battered poly sled behind him made a rasping racket skipping and bouncing across the rough ice. Seagull's deep-blue ice fishing shelter loomed larger as Davecki trudged along. Skidding the sled to a stop outside the zipped shut tent door, the low hiss of the propane heater inside the shelter filtered through the rip stop fabric to Davecki's not quite numb ears.

"'Lo," came Seagull's guttural greeting from inside the tent. "'Bout time you showed up, hoser."

Outside the tent's flap, Davecki studied five medium-sized crappies frozen on the ice like frosty green pancakes. The sixth fish was ten-or-so-inches nose to tail, an excellent future supper involving beer batter and a smoking-hot cast iron skillet. Gotta talk him out of that one, Davecki thought.

He took a final scan of the pines and oaks of Pedderson Point on the right side of the channel to Lake Minerva, they pointed toward Mickaud Point on the left. There, the low scrub of alder and tamarack along the shore melded into the higher crest of ground where the floor-to-ceiling windows of the Ancient Pines Lodge glowed yellow amongst the old growth white and Norway pines that survived the decades of wind, ice storms, and—miracle of miracles—the rampage of the Hines Lumber Company in the late eighteen hundreds.

"You ain't getting that big one," Seagull's raspy voice oozed through the 900-denier fabric.

"Moi?" Davecki asked, "I catch my own, don't cha know."

"Right," Raspy Voice slithered through the tent wall.

Davecki grabbed a lawn chair from the sled and unzipped the flap. A gush of humid air smacked him in the face. Inside, the mesh of the heater sitting in the middle of the circle of fishing holes glowed orange like a tiny fossil-fuel sun. A small pool of dark water shimmered under the heater, its black gas hose trailed away under the tent's sidewall looking like a thick snake slithering to the propane tank outside. The enormous occupant testing the structural integrity of a flimsy looking lawn chair didn't glance at the newcomer. His entire attention focused on the sonar fish finder beside the ice hole.

"You want me to wear a mask?" Davecki asked.

Seagull cocked his head toward Davecki. His big bushy beard did its best to follow. The gesture looked like a Bernese Mountain Dog asking a question. "Seriously? Out here? Ice fishing? The plandemic doesn't play out here, man."

Davecki unfolded his chair. He placed it near the hole farthest from Seagull's that had a second sonar unit. He studied the sonar, its red flashes sharing the secrets of the lake-bottom thirty-six feet down. "Plenty of fish."

"Yeah. I'd switch from mealies to a minnow," Seagull groused.

"Bite fell off in anticipation of your arrival. Thanks for that."

Davecki grunted. He picked up the miniature fishing rod and reel, raised and lowered the rig. The blaze green bobber in the hole jigged and shuddered as he tempted the fish below. The flasher shifted around indicating the bait's movement. "Be nice if the wallies started."

"You wish. Maybe after dark."

Davecki dragged the bobber stopper up the monofilament line a foot or so. "Gonna try moving closer to the bottom."

"Good luck with that. Crappies are higher."

"Right," Davecki lowered the line. The flasher showed the bait descending. He jigged it, feeling the line slacken as it touched bottom and tighten as he raised it up again. He repeated the exercise in the silence of the tent, the hiss of the propane heater the only sound. He sent *I'm hungry* mental messages to the little fishy brains below.

Davecki snuck a glance at the master fisherman on the other side of the tent. Seagull was born big, grew up big, played both left guard and defensive lineman at Southeastern Shore High, and, in middle age, grew to overfill the air-ride seat of the big Peterbilt logging truck he drove. It would be nice for once to become worthy of the self-appointed master fisherman's approval, Davecki thought.

Patience, he thought. The propane heater hissed. Seagull's chair squeaked. Patience. Jig. Jig. Jig. Should concede to Seagull's superiority and switch bait. Patience, he thought.

"You know," Seagull grumbled. "With this Covid business, I should kick your butt outside. Shouldn't be sharing a tent with you. Perfect virus incubator environment in here."

Jig. Jig. Jig. "I can skedaddle if you want," Davecki said.

"Naw. No biggie," Seagull said. "Gotta wonder, though."

Nibble. Nibble. The line quivered. Wait for it, he calmed himself. Wait. "Wonder what?" Davecki asked.

"How the pandemic thing came about."

Come on little fishy, bite, Davecki sent thoughts down into the hole. "That's no biggie," Davecki said.

"Really? Do tell," Seagull said.

"Winneboujou and Nanabozho made a bet."

"Not more of your Trickster stuff."

"I've got a nibble down low, Mr. Master Fisherman. Okay, if it pleases you, Zuckerberg and Bezos made a bet. Come on little fishy, bite," Davecki said.

"What kind of bet?"

"One bet the other that they could have all of America wearing masks inside a year."

"You're crazy. You do know that, don't you?"

"Crazy like a fox!" Davecki said as he jerked the rod up. "Fish on!"

"Humpf," from Master Fisherman.

Lifting rod and reeling in, Davecki said, "Feels like a nice one."

"Any fish you catch is a nice one."

Davecki lifted and reeled, drawing the fish to the surface. The chair behind scraped and squawked as Seagull moved to observe the catch coming out of the hole.

"Holy mackerel!" Davecki yelled as the microlight rod bent double, the tip of the pole diving for the ice hole like a water witcher's wand. He kneeled forward out of his chair, following the rod toward the hole as the monofilament line hissed out of the spool.

"Must be a northern or muskie hit the sunny!" Seagull yelped. "Don't let the line break!"

"Ya think?!" Davecki stuck the tip of the bent rod down into the hole, plunging the rig all the way up to the open face of the spinning reel to keep the thin line away from the sharp edges of the ice hole.

"Easy! Easy!" Seagull said as he scuttled on his knees toward the action. "Let 'em go. Let 'em run."

"My hands are freezing," Davecki said.

"Suffer, hoser, suffer," Seagull said. He snatched the sonar out of the way, the bulbous sending unit splashed out of the water like a seal surfacing.

The spool stopped humming. Davecki eased the rod back out of the hole.

"Let 'em chow down," Seagull said.

"'K," Davecki said. He took one hand off the rod and reel, wiped it on his Carhartt bibs.

"Keep hold of that thing," Seagull admonished. "He'll rip it right out of your hands if he decides to make another run."

"He better not, line's almost gone," Davecki said, tipping the reel sideways to get a look at the spool. "My heart's beating a hundred miles an hour."

"No kidding. Mine too."

"No way we're going to get him up with this light line."

"Just be patient and don't go jerking hard. That Superline is tough. Try to keep it away from the edge of the ice. Just take your time and ease him up. He'll figure out that something's wrong and make another run or three. He'll tire out and come along peacefully."

Davecki glanced at Seagull and wondered if the grizzled trucker/fisherman realized what he'd just said. Come along peacefully. Wonder how many times I said that during my career.

"See if you can nudge him up a little."

Davecki eased up the rod. The tip bent downward.

"Don't break that rod in half," Seagull said.

"I got this, Seagull," Davecki snipped.

"Okay. Okay. Lighten up, man. Just keep easing him up. Gain as much line as you can."

"Better lighten the drag," Davecki said, twisting the tension knob on the reel.

"Better get some light going," Seagull said. He knee-walked to a green and battered two-bag lantern, fired it up and hung it from the hook at the top center of the tent. Davecki winced away from the white glow. His eyes burned. The smell of uncombusted hydrocarbons stung his nose.

Whenever the fish got close to the hole, it took off again, unspooling the line with a hot sizzle. While no giant marlin like in *The Old Man and the Sea,* the beast below tired. Then a sharp nose appeared through the ten-inch hole. "Muskie!" Seagull cried. He grabbed the monster by the gills. "Sweet!" he hollered as the 40-inch fish slithered up through the hole.

"Holy mackerel!" Davecki yelled.

"No! Holy muskie!" Seagull said.

"Wow!"

"Look at that big beautiful bastard!" Seagull said, as he flopped the fish out on the ice. The giant jaws opened and closed. The gills pulsed as the fish searched for oxygen. The long strong body arched; the wide tail fin strained upwards off the ice.

"Season's over for muskie," Seagull said, "better get him back in the water fast."

"Gotta get a picture," Davecki said, fishing for his phone.

Seagull leaned to the tackle box, grabbed needle nose pliers and snipped the line. "What the heck is this?" he asked, running his wet fingers along the fish's flank. Seagull ran his fingers over an obvious bump the size of a tangerine that bulged up from the fish's side.

"Tumor?" Davecki asked as he took pics, the flash bursting light all around the tent.

"Knock it off with those flashes," Seagull said. He pushed on the fishy flank. "Could be. Feels hard."

Davecki ran his hand across the fish's belly. "Holy mackerel. What is that?"

"Only one way to find out," Seagull said.

"But...season's over. What if the wardens come?"

"They're too busy chasing drunk snowmobilers."

Seagull grabbed the fish knocker from the tackle box and rapped the fish a good one on the head. The mighty body curled upward in a last attempt at life. Fumbling a knife from the tackle box, he slit up the gut. The belly spilled out. Seagull sliced it open.

"Holy mackerel!" Davecki cried, as a slick and slimy golden watch popped out of the gut.

"Quit saying that!" Seagull said as he hefted the watch toward the light.

"Sorry. Sorry."

The watch gleamed yellow in the white light as Seagull smudged slime and the most recent muskie meal of bluegill parts from the face and back. The twist-o-flex type band dripped goo as Seagull bent it aside. He bent over and sloshed the watch in the water of the open hole from which the muskie had come.

"Hold on to it!" Davecki chirped.

"Lighten up man. I got this," Seagull said as he swished and sloshed the watch clean.

"I can't believe he ate the whole thing!"

"Will you look at that, it's still ticking," Seagull said.

"Just like a Timex," Davecki said, smirking. "Takes a licking and keeps on ticking."

Seagull shot Davecki a withering glance, drew the watch close to his face. "Holy mack...," he stopped himself, "...This thing's a Rolex."

"You're kidding. Right?" Davecki asked.

"Never kid a kidder," Seagull said. He inverted the band, squinted, said, "There's writing on the back." Pushing it away, he said, "Wish I had my readers. Can't see what the inscription says."

"It must have been time consuming to eat the whole thing."

"Dave!"

"Sorry. Sorry."

Seagull shook the watch free of drips again and handed it to Davecki. "Can you read what it says?"

Davecki repeated the focal length exercise, drawing the watch close and moving it farther away. "Need longer arms."

"Hell getting old," Seagull said.

"Tell me about it. I know who to call."

Davecki extracted his phone. "Dang," he said, lifting it toward the tent's roof. "Why is the reception so bad?"

"Sunspots," Seagull answered.

"Maybe there's better reception outside."

"You just keep dreaming that dream," Seagull said.

Davecki exited, called out, "Dang it! No signal!"

"It's a sign, Dave," Seagull said through the tent wall.

"Of what?"

"No need to get the law involved."

"I'm not getting the law involved," Davecki said as he re-entered the tent. "I'm just calling someone with better eyeballs than either of us."

"Right. Stanski needs readers too, man."

"Well, then he'll have a pair or three in his squad," Davecki said.

Back in his chair, Seagull stared at the Vexilar screen, rocked forth and back, the aluminum legs squeaking on the ice. "Quit trying to call Stanski. I got a magnifying glass back at the shack that will do the job just fine. I'll throw in that big crappie as a closer."

"What's your problem, Seagull? It's no crime to find a watch in a muskie. Weird. But nothing illegal."

"You forgetting the season's closed?"

"Well, there's that. But we can afford to pay the fine now," Davecki said. He waved the Rolex toward Seagull.

Finally glancing from the sonar, Seagull said, "It's gotta be a knock-off."

"Good things can happen as well as bad, Seagull. Some New York hedge fund manager was on a fishing trip last summer and dropped his watch overboard. The big fish saw it and struck it like it was a crank bait squirming through the water."

"Humpf. If that thing has been in its belly since summer all it would be is muskie poop by now."

Davecki studied Seagull, "What's your problem, man?"

"Nothing."

"Spill, man."

"Hayward quit taking wood two weeks ago."

"Seriously? What happened?"

"You ever hear of a little thing called Coronavirus?"

"Yeah, but isn't logging an essential service?"

Seagull twisted his big bull neck, studied Davecki. "Sometimes I think you're from another planet or just plain stupid."

"Well. You got that right. The stupid part, anyway. I hear people are making more on unemployment than if they were working."

Seagull grunted. "Ain't no unemployment for me, pal."

"What? You're kidding."

Seagull shook his bushy beard, "I'm an independent contractor, man."

"You got savings, right?"

"I wish," Seagull said, his gaze fell upon the Rolex. His bush-like eyebrows scrunched together, making a unibrow.

"Here," Davecki said, tossing the watch. "You can have it. I'll take the big crappie."

Seagull grabbed at the watch, missed the catch. He had played lineman, not wide receiver. The watch flew toward one of the open holes in the ice.

"No!" Davecki yelled as he dove like Jacques Plante in goal, swatting the watch away from the black hole at the last second. It skidded to a stop at the scuffed steel toe of Seagull's enormous camo boot.

"Nice save, man," Seagull said. He picked up the watch and studied it again.

Recovering from his dive, Davecki checked his pocket. "At least my phone didn't fall out and fall in," he said, extracting the phone. "I'm going to hike out to good reception."

"Big mistake, pal. But it's a free country." Seagull extended the watch toward Davecki. No tossing now. "You caught the fish. It's your watch, man."

"You sure?"

"Sure as shite, man."

Davecki took the watch, turned to leave, stopped, eyeballed Seagull, said, "I got a load of firewood from Tall Timbers last week. You could dice it up. Twenty bucks an hour."

Seagull studied Davecki for a few seconds. "How many cords?"

"I paid for twelve."

"Twelve? Take me 'til spring, man. I'm outta shape." Seagull grinned.

"Bull. Five hundred max. For the whole job. Cut, split, stacked and covered."

"You paying worker's comp? I might get injured on the job."

"You? Mr. World Champion Chainsaw Man? Right. Deal or no?"

Seagull sighed. Picked up his fishing rod. Started reeling. "Deal."

"You calling it quits?"

"Nope. I'm putting on a big treble hook with ten sinkers. Maybe I can snag the rich guy's wallet full of money. That's gotta be down there somewhere."

"It could be a purse, man."

"Yeah. Right. I forgot," Seagull sighed.

"I'll be back for the sled shortly."

"Everything you do is shortly," the big man said.

CHAPTER 2

Halfway back to the landing, Davecki got two bars.

"You're in luck. I'm on Sand Spit Road. I can be there in a couple of minutes," Deputy Patrick Stanski said.

The Hayfield County Dodge Charger Squad descending the boat landing turned access road in the winter resembled a powdered donut, caked as it was with the D.O.T.'s favorite condiment, road salt. The fancy SHERIFF logo and decals promising to protect and serve were mostly obscured by the chalk-like overcoating. The passenger window powered down. The glow from the instrument panel and the open laptop radiated yellow, blue and red, the modern constellations guiding the lone patrolman through the night. "Hop in," Stanski said as he clutched a fistful of papers from the passenger seat.

"You ever hear of a clipboard?" Davecki asked, settling in.

"That some sort of newfangled labor-saving device?"

"Just invented. Your department can't afford one?"

"Piff! Who needs a clipboard with one of these?" Stanski said, tapping the keyboard of the laptop mounted between them. "Tell me about this watch business again."

"Nothing more to tell," Davecki said, pulling the watch from his pocket. "Caught a muskie that hit on the bluegill I was reeling in. There was a Rolex in its gut. Same as I said on the phone." He rolled the watch in a circle between his two hands, watching the gold flicker.

"You think something's fishy, right?"

Davecki sighed. "Stan, you need to leave the puns to the professionals."

"Why should they have all the fin?"

"Because, on a scale of one to ten, your puns are unfathomable."

Stanski, refusing to look at Davecki, said, "Muskie you always put my puns down?"

"Dear Cod, help me," Davecki said.

"You called me just for the halibut, then? This isn't an oFISHal visit?"

Davecki sighed, "You're krilling me, Stan." He continued to twirl the watch between his fishy-smelling fingers.

"You've got me hooked. Now quit squidding around. Let me see that dang watch."

"Say please, Stan."

"This is such a pile of carp…."

Davecki grinned, kept twiddling the watch.

Stanski caved. "Please?"

"Who's a good boy?" Davecki said, handing the watch across the glowing laptop.

Stanski held the watch up. "This thing stinks." He inverted the band, squinted, asked, "You read this inscription yet?"

"No. That's why I called you, nimrod."

"My readers are back at the station," Stanski said. Grinning, he tossed the watch back at Davecki, saying, "Hold on."

Stanski tromped his foot down on the gas pedal. The AWD

made the squad leap like a scared kitty on a YouTube video. Stanski spun the steering wheel. The car shuddered and lurched across the rough ice like a four-thousand-pound ballerina making a wide churning circle. The engine screamed. The exhaust sounded like thunder.

"WOO HOO!" Stanski hollered.

Davecki snatched the watch out of the air with his left hand and grabbed the handgrip on the door with his right.

Stanski completed the power turn and pointed the halogen lights back up the landing road from whence he came.

"Way to ruin my wilderness experience, Stan. What the heck was that about?" Davecki asked.

"No reason. Just having a little fun. These long nights get boring. Can you believe we survived all those winter patrols without All Wheel Drive?"

"Tell me about it."

The car bounced up the landing. Stanski braked to a rapid stop next to Davecki's F-150.

Grabbing the door latch, Davecki said, "See you at the station."

"Roger."

All four tires spit ice shards and rocks at Davecki as the bored patrolman punched the Dodge again. Bits of ice and gravel splatted on Davecki's Carhartts and pinged off the paint and thin, rusting, sheet metal of the F-150 behind him. Wish I could have studded tires, Davecki thought.

CHAPTER 3

The aroma of pizza infused the atmosphere of the Sheriff Department's satellite station. A red and white checked Iron Creek Pizzeria box with one slice remaining sat in the middle of the brown and round table that sat in the middle of the room that sat in the middle of the shanty that Homeland Security built.

"Gonna be a cold one tonight," Davecki said, hunching his shoulders. Flakes of snow fell from his Carhartt jacket. "That looks good. How old is it?" he asked, nodding at the pizza.

"Every pizza from them is good. It was there when I signed on this afternoon," Stanski said. He walked to a cluttered desk in the corner, snatched a pair of reading glasses off the paperwork thereupon.

Davecki plucked the pizza from the box, sniffed it. "Smells great." He bit the pointy end off. Chewing with an appreciative look on his face, he further declared around the food, "Shelly sure makes great pizza."

"Let me have it, Dave," Stanski said as he sat at the round table. He hung his readers on his delicate nose and shoved the pizza box aside.

Davecki extended the pizza.

"The watch, doofus."

Davecki grinned, dug the watch out of his Carhartt. Handed it over.

Adjusting the watch to the overhead lighting, Stanski moved it forth and back to get the focal length right. "I wonder who would throw an expensive watch like this into Husky Bay."

"Nobody, doofus," Davecki said. "Plus there's nine lakes in the chain, dipwad. That musky could have gobbled the watch anywhere at any time."

"Maybe it slipped off a rich guy's wrist when he dove off their Bennington pontoon," Stanski said.

"Or a rich woman."

"There's that," Stanski said. He tilted the watch some more, squinted some more, said, "There we go." He moved his lips like a monk mouthing prayers. Squinted some more. "Huh."

"Alright already, jerk. What's it say?"

Stanski moved the watch away a little. "Having a hard time reading it with all the fish slime."

"Come on, dipstick."

Stanski looked across the table at Davecki, smirked, said, "It's just a bunch of numbers."

"That's it?"

Stanski moved the watch around, seeking better light. "You need hearing aids or something?"

Davecki stood up, shrugged out of his Carhartt jacket and hung it on the back of his chair. "What are they?"

Stanski answered, "65878190 above 149778943."

"Huh. Read 'em again," Davecki said. He extracted the pen from the sleeve pocket of the Carhartt.

"65878190149778943."

"I'm going to have to kill you, Stan. Slowly, please." Davecki pulled the pizza box over.

"You should sign on as an auxiliary. That way you could go to the new classes on use of force." Stanski read the numbers again.

Davecki wrote the numbers on the box. He said, "I thought the police were being defunded. They can afford training?"

"Spare no expense turning bad cops into social workers," Stanski said. "Seriously, Dave, you should come to work for us. We need fresh flesh. Except in your case the flesh would be necrotic. We could all call you Decrepit Deputy Dave."

"Necrotic? You reading autopsies again?" He studied the numbers. The string of numbers looked like musical notes launching out of the Pizza-man caricature printed on the box. "These things might be lat-longs."

"Seriously?" Stanski reexamined the watch.

Davecki fished out his phone. He poked at the phone face, asked, "What's the password here?"

"Countymountie and some numbers."

"And the numbers are...."

"I commit a lot of things to memory, but not those numbers. They're written on the Norvado box," Stanski said, shrugging toward the white box with green flashing lights on the wall.

Davecki went to the wall, squinted at the Sharpie-inscribed password and poked it in. "You know that Norvado stands for north and fast?" he asked.

"You commit that to memory? Something's wrong with you, man."

"Sometimes stuff just sticks. Something's wrong with you."

Stanski flipped the watch back to its face. "Wonder if this thing's real or a knock-off?"

Davecki walked back to the table and sat, all while swiping and reading the screen. "Huh," he said three times.

Stanski shook his head. "A gunshot to the kidney area will make death slow and painful."

"Huh. Interesting." Davecki focused on the phone.

"Don't make me break leather, man."

Davecki grinned, turned from the phone, "It's Alaska."

"Really?"

Davecki grinned, reached the phone across the table, said, "There we go." He waved the screen toward Stanski, moving it in circles.

Stanski glared.

"It's all on the map right there in front of you, Stan."

More glaring.

"You're no fun," Davecki said, retracting the phone. "It's north of Fairbanks. North of a place called Livingood."

"Thank you," Stanski said.

Davecki resumed swiping and pinching the screen. "Interesting."

"I swear, Dave, I'll get Seagull to strangle you."

Davecki smirked, said, "Guess those use of force classes worked. Just get someone else to apply the hold. Besides, Seagull couldn't catch me. Me too fast. He too fat."

"Then a bullet will have to do. You can't outrun a bullet."

"True," Davecki said as he continued to swipe the phone screen. "But, with your aim, I could zig and zag and survive to file the police brutality lawsuit."

"Dead men can't sue."

"They'll love you in Waupun."

"What's so interesting?" Stanski asked.

"It's in the middle of nowhere on what looks to be a mining claim according to Alaska Mapper."

Stanski's shoulder mic hissed. A female voice asked, "Stan? You there?"

Keying the mic, he said, "Ten-four, Michelle. What's up?"

The voice from the tiny dancer on his shoulder said, "Mrs. Korjela called. The snowmobilers are at it again."

"Ten-four. I'll check it out."

Stanski looked at Davecki's face glowing white from the phone's radiation melting multiple millions of brain cells. "Damn snowmobilers can't stay on the trail for some reason. They're running over her pine plantation. With this much snow this year, they probably think it's an open field."

"I see," Davecki said.

"There's signs posted, but there's plenty of sledders who could care less."

"Yup."

Stanski stared at Davecki staring at his phone. "Hawthorne said she thinks you're adorable."

"Uh huh."

Smirking, Stanski said, "There's been another outbreak of Covid-19 in Hayfield County, 79 dead."

"That's nice."

"Lord, help me."

"Umm. Oh. Sorry, Stan. Sorry," Davecki said, looking away from the screen at last. "I expanded the Mapper at the coordinates and a claim number came up. I cut and pasted the number into Google and a federal mining lease came up."

"So?"

"So, don't you have to get going to Korjela's?" Davecki kept poking at the phone screen.

"So you *were* listening."

"More or less."

Stanski sighed, "Nah. The sleds will be long gone by the time I get there. The Crick Dicks on their fancy Skandics will have to chase 'em down."

"A true public servant."

"Thanks."

Davecki said, "The Alaska Mining Claims Map says that the leaseholder is Carczak Gold. There's a P.O. Box in Fairbanks."

"No kidding?" Stanski said. He pulled out his own phone. He poked once.

"Seriously," Davecki said.

Stanski put the phone to his ear, waited a bit, said, "Yeah. Hi, Mrs. K. This is Deputy Stanski. Everything okay out there now?" He listened a bit. Nodded his head. Looked at Davecki. Grinned. Said, "Okay. Excellent. No. No problem. Call anytime. The wardens will take care of it. Say hi to Ern." He lowered the phone, poked it. "There you go, smarty pants. To protect and serve."

"You have her on speed dial?"

"She's a nice lady. Deserves the best the County has to offer."

"Huh," Davecki said, looking at his phone again.

"What?"

"According to the Alaska Department of Finance records, Carczak Gold is incorporated at Highland Road, Eagle River. President is John Wayne Carczak. Veep is Thomas Richard Harrison. Secretary-Treasurer is Molly Carczak. "

"Now that *is* interesting," Stanski said.

"How so?"

"It's a long story," Stanski said. "I'll make coffee."

CHAPTER 4

"How's Hawthorne, by the way?" Davecki asked, as Stanski held the stack of white ribbed coffee filters to the light above the sink.

"How in the world is a person supposed to use just one filter at a time when they pack them in so tight?" Stanski stuffed a filter into the black plastic basket. "Hawthorne? Who's Hawthorne?"

"Right," Davecki said. "You know, gorgeous FBI agent. Lowly rural deputy love interest?"

"Oh, her. Haven't talked to her in a couple of weeks. She's working undercover on Lac du Flambeau. You wouldn't believe the huge sums of taxpayer money she's losing at blackjack just to bust a couple of wasted meth heads."

"Right. So, what's with Carczak Gold?"

Slowly, silently, Stan trickled the silver sliver of water into the back of the black plastic coffee maker.

Serenity now. Serenity now, Davecki rehearsed Frank Costanza's mantra.

"You're no fun," Stanski said. He flipped the flap shut on the maker, clicked the on button, returned to the table, plunked down, said, "Okay. You win. Back in the Sixties there was a bum named John Wayne Carczak. Everyone called him Jack. He had a pal named Harry Harrison. They were bad news in every which way. Drugs, drink, and dirty deeds. The crime rate for the entire county went down by two-thirds when they stole Sulu Panula's Dodge Power Wagon and lit out for Alaska."

"Who in their right mind would steal a Power Wagon, let alone drive it up the Alcan? Those things rode like a Conestoga."

"Couple of losers. But, something must have gone right," Stanski said. He picked up the watch, studied it. "I'm guessing a watch like this has to be a couple grand at least."

"Humpf," Davecki said. "You know, there should be a *Sixty Minutes* show or something warning mothers not to middle name their kid Wayne."

"Why's that?" Stanski put the watch down.

"The name John Wayne Gacy ring a bell?"

"Oh, yeah. Right, the Wayne theory."

The door behind Davecki opened.

"Look what the cat dragged in," Stanski said, chin nodding toward the incoming Seagull.

"You guys aren't going to believe this," Seagull said as he back-kicked the thin door shut with a powerful boost from his size sixteen boot heel. He waved his phone in the dynamic duo's direction.

"That's a pretty fancy phone for an out-of-work trucker," Davecki said.

"Got it for free for switching plans."

"What won't we believe?" Stanski asked.

"By the way, hoser. I brought your sled back for you." Seagull plucked the watch off the table, raised and lowered it before his eyes. "Yup. I was right."

"Thanks, Seagull. You're a saint," Davecki said. "Will you get to the point please?"

Seagull glanced at Davecki, swung his gaze to Stanski. "What's bugging him?"

"Must be low blood sugar or something. He just scarfed a week-old piece of pizza and said it was tasty."

"What!?" Davecki yelped. "You said it was there when you came on shift this afternoon."

"That's what I said. What I didn't say was that it's been there for every log-on for the last week. Your cop training is gone to seed. Trust but verify, pal."

"Jerk. Seven days?"

"Well, maybe one or two."

"Jerk. It was still delicious."

"Yeah, Shelly's pizza is great, hot, cold, fresh or old," Seagull said.

Stanski and Davecki eyeballed Seagull who raised his eyebrows, "What? What?"

Stanski and Davecki looked at each other, said simultaneously, "Poet and don't know it."

"Anyway, if we can dispense with the inside jokes for a second, I have big news," Seagull said. "Umm, that coffee smells good." Seagull eyeballed the coffee maker and moved toward the cupboard. He moved glacially, slowly even.

"By the way," Stanski said, "I bought the pizza just before signing on an hour ago."

"I'm going to have to kill you, Stan," Davecki said.

"You can dish it out but can't take it, huh," Stanski said.

"Well, there is that," Davecki said.

Stanski smirked at Davecki, looked at Seagull, said, "Spill, Seagull. Spill."

"Wouldn't want to spoil a good lover's quarrel," Seagull said.

"He's toying with us, Stan. What we gonna do with the body?"

"I could get the County's big chipper and grind him up like in Fargo."

"Ugh. Too messy," Davecki said.

"Feed him to the fishes?"

"I'm not chopping a hole in the ice big enough to get him through."

"Drag his carcass behind a snowmobile until there's nothing left but a frayed knot in the rope?"

"'Fraid not," Davecki answered. "Too many body parts all along the Corregidor Trail."

"You two are too tense," Seagull said, laughing as he poured himself coffee. "Geez, this stuff looks like tar. How old is it?"

Davecki raised a hand to Stanski, "Don't answer that!"

"Sheesh, Dave. Lighten up. Seagull, would you please tell us what your big news is?" Stanski asked.

"Pretty please," Davecki added.

"I win," Seagull said, grinning. "Well, before, in the tent, when I looked at the watch, I thought it said Daytona on the face. But I wasn't sure. Who can see in that light and with no readers? The bite was off so I got to surfing on Rolex watches and guess what?"

"I thought there were solar flares ruining the signal out there," Davecki said.

"I have a better phone than you," Seagull said.

"Together we could take him," Stanski suggested.

"In your dreams," Seagull said, adding, "That thing's worth two mil. Maybe more."

"What?" Cop and ex-cop said.

"I'm just relaying what the Internet says."

Davecki plucked the watch from the table. "MINE!"

Seagull said, "Remember you caught that in my tent, pal."

"Now, boys. Let's not get too far ahead of ourselves," Stanski said, adding, "It's gotta be a knock-off anyway."

"Going to have to get it appraised," Seagull said. "Hand it over, Dave."

"You're not going anywhere with my watch," Davecki said.

"That watch is evidence, mister. Hand it over," Stanski said.

"Ain't no crime catching a muskie," Seagull said.

"It is when muskie season is over," Stanski said. "I got Warden Dan on speed dial too."

"He's the one who caught it," Seagull said, nodding toward Davecki, "he's the lawbreaker."

"ME?! You killed it and cut it open," Davecki defended.

"Then you're both under arrest," Stanski said.

Man Mountain and ex-dick stared at Stanski. Then they slow-looked at each other before bursting out laughing.

Stanski held his firm and serious look as long as he could, then he joined the laughter. "Okay. Okay. You two fight it out."

Seagull said, "I'm starving. Haven't eaten since breakfast. I filleted those crappies. Got any flour in this dump?"

"What about the muskie?" Davecki asked.

"Freezing stiff as a board in the back of the truck as we speak," Seagull said.

"Flour? Of course. Every wilderness outpost of law and order has flour. It's on the top of every checklist for essential law enforcement equipment."

"Now who needs to lighten up?" Davecki asked.

Stanski smirked, "Well, ask a stupid question…."

"Who you calling stupid?" Seagull said.

"You, big fella. What you going to do about it?"

"Now boys," Davecki said. "I don't want to have to restrain you both."

It was Seagull and Stanski's turn to slow-look before bursting into laughter.

"I could. I could," Davecki said. "I'm a seasoned professional highly trained in the use of force. I'm like Tom Cruise playing Jack Reacher. Don't mess with me."

"I look like Tom Cruise, right?" Stanski said.

"You're more like Quasimodo," Seagull said.

"Guess we're going to have to eat sushi," Davecki said.

"You guys are real pals," Stanski said. "It just so happens that there is some confiscated flour in the back room. So there."

"You confiscated flour?" Davecki asked.

"What he said," Seagull said, tilting his head at Davecki while staring at Stanski.

"Yeah, when there's cocaine hidden in it."

"Sweet," Seagull said.

"Not only flour, there's some confiscated Brule Beer too. We can make beer batter," Stanski said. He pushed back from the table, headed for the rear door. "The frying pan is in the cupboard above the microwave."

"Yum," Seagull said as he headed for the front door. "Be right back with the protein."

Davecki put the Rolex on the table and went for the cupboard. Wonder if that thing is going to get me from the frying pan to the fire, he wondered.

CHAPTER 5

"Umm, this is delicious," Davecki said, smacking his lips and wiping same with the back of his hand. "What else do you know about John Wayne Carczak?"

"It was one of my first cases when I joined the county. Carczak and Harrison were petty thieves. Carczak went by the nickname Carjack, sponged off his wife Molly while running wild with Harrison. She was a veterinarian. Paid his bills. Covered his fines."

"Classic enabler," Seagull said.

Stanski raised an eyeball in Seagull's direction, "That court-mandated AA gig sticking, huh?"

"Has its merits." Seagull shrugged his broad shoulders. "I'm getting a lot of good stuff reading Deepchat Chopra these days."

Stanski looked at Davecki.

Davecki shook his head, "You mean Deepak Chopra?"

"Yeah, him." Seagull added, "And Oprah. They're teaching me how to medicate."

Davecki looked at Stanski. "Your turn."

Stanski shook his head, "You mean meditate?"

"Yeah, that. It's helping me survive this pandemic."

Stanski and Davecki shook their heads.

"Anyway, Carczak's wife was the responsible type. She paid the way while the losers robbed vacant cabins and lake-property garages in the winter when nobody was around. Stole the occasional easy-picking snowmobile from bar parking lots when the key was in the ignition. Dealt marijuana to their pals. One day Sulu from Oulu reported his Power Wagon stolen. Case went unsolved for a few weeks, concurrent with a significant drop in the county crime rate. The mystery was solved when the Alaska State Police called asking about a Power Wagon and Carczak, who claimed that the vehicle was his uncle's in Wisconsin."

"You got all these details down pretty good, bro," Seagull said. He stabbed another crappie fillet from the frying pan in the middle of the table, transferring it to his empty plate.

"You always remember your first case," Stanski forked the last fillet from the now empty pan.

"Hey!" Davecki said. "I'm still hungry."

"You snooze. You lose," Stanski said.

"What happened up in Alaska?" Davecki asked.

Stanski coaxed his words out past a mouthful of crappie, "Who knows for sure. We were glad those two were Alaska's problem and Sulu never did like that Power Wagon." He was about to say more when his shoulder mic squawked.

"Stan. You there?" Michelle's voice sparked out of the tiny black box hanging from his epaulet.

Stanski reached up, keyed the mic, said, "Yeah, Michelle. What's up?"

"Lady out on Little Mountain Road says the snowmobilers are racing again."

Stanski keyed the mic, "Ten-four. I'll head over there."

"Roger."

Stanski got up, grinned, said, "Sorry to leave you guys to clean up, but duty calls."

"Why not let the wardens on their Skandics handle this one too?" Davecki asked.

"Because there's dishes to do," Seagull said.

"You so smart," Stanski said.

"You got remote start on that thing?" Davecki said.

"Yup."

"Sheesh," Seagull said. "I'm going to have to apply for a deputy's job."

"Want to ride along, Dave?"

"Ab-so-surely," Davecki said. He grabbed his Carhartt off the back of his chair, snatched the watch off the table, stuck it in his left jacket pocket and followed Stanski to the front door.

"Make sure you wipe that frying pan down good before you leave, loser," Stanski said over his back.

Seagull reached over, grabbed Stanski's plate and tipped the half-eaten fillet onto his own.

In the squad, Davecki said, "You were going to say more about Carczak."

"Pretty interesting. About ten years went by and who should call again? Alaska. Wanting contact info about Carczak's next of kin. They found a pickup and a black lab abandoned in a parking lot in the Wrangells. Registered to Molly Carczak."

"What about Carczak?"

"Vanished. No trace. They figured a bear got him. Or he fell hiking in the mountains."

"No kidding?"

"Never kid a kidder."

Stanski reached over to the open laptop between them, punched a key and said, "Harrison turned up a year or so later. The general population got lucky when he shot a guy over Cass Lake way and got sent up."

"Killed him?"

"Yeah. Drug deal gone bad."

Davecki felt for the watch. Shifted it around with his fingers through the thick duck canvas of the Carhartt slash pocket. "If the watch is worth two mil, it's a big loss to somebody."

"Well, yeah, the insurance company."

"There's that."

Stanski turned on Hipster Road heading toward Little Mountain. Ahead, the wild gyrations of bouncing snowmobile headlights approaching. "Damn ditch riders," he said. "Why can't people stay on the groomed trails?" He punched the button that turned the squad from a regular car into a flashing display of red strobe lights worthy of a state holiday tree. He braked to a stop, angling the squad across the road. He got out of the car just as the snowmobiler whizzed past in the ditch.

"Dirtbag!" he hollered, falling back into his seat.

"Very effective, officer."

"Desist, Dave," he said, throwing the shifter into reverse, tromping the gas, spinning the wheel and making the car do Baryshnikov again. Stanski kept the power on as the car straightened out with the reverse spin of the steering wheel. Just as he dropped the gearbox into drive, another snowmobile screamed past, red lights flashing.

"Huh, will you look at that," Davecki said. "Hard to believe these new snowmobiles are faster than most cars." As he spoke, another sled scorched past, red lights flashing.

Stanski said. "Guess the Crick Dicks got this one too. Those guys get around."

"May as well get me back, Stan. I can help Seagull with the dishes."

"You think he'll actually do them?" Stanski asked as the squad retraced its tracks back toward town.

"I'll make sure he does. Or, if he ditched, I'll do 'em myself. So, Harrison goes to the stir. How long a hitch?"

"Not sure. Probably fifteen years." Stanski said.

"For killing a guy?"

Stanski huffed, "If he'd shot his wife, he'd have got probation."

"No kidding," Davecki said. "Well, something's up with this thing." He dug the watch out from the Carhartt pocket and flashed it around in the dim light from the laptop and instrument cluster.

"Ya think?" Stanski wagged his head.

In front of the sub-station, Stanski put the Dodge Squad in park. "Seagull's truck's still here. Probably drank all the confiscated beer."

"He's okay. He's laid off." Davecki popped his door open. The cold December air clawed in like a cat climbing a screen.

"That's no big loss with all the money the government is giving away these days," Stanski said.

"You're a compassionate type, you know that Stan?"

"We cops are here to serve. Now get out. It's freezing in here all of a sudden."

Davecki exited the squad and headed for the station without closing the Dodge Squad's door.

"VERY FUNNY!" Stanski hollered from within. He jammed the car into drive, punched the throttle. The squad leapt forward. The passenger door self-slammed as Davecki dodged flying stones and ice chunks thrown up by the four spinning stud-infested tires.

Seagull's broad back was at the sink. He said nothing as Davecki shrugged out of his Carhartt and hung it on the same chair as before. He moved beside Seagull and pulled a dirty-gray-from-overuse towel strung through the handle of a drawer. He picked up a plate. As he dried he wondered, maybe I should get a new phone for free. Drying a fork he asked, "How in the world is a watch worth two mil?"

"The Internet says that Odell wore one worth two million to a game."

"Really?" Davecki asked, holding a knife up to the light. "Missed a chunk," he said, handing the knife back to the dishwasher.

"Paul Newman's Rolex brought almost eighteen million." Seagull thumb-nailed the chunk of food off the knife, handed it back without washing it.

"If it's worth two million, you won't have to worry about not getting unemployment benefits," Davecki said, tossing the knife in the open silverware drawer.

"Huh," Seagull grunted. His thick, blonde, going-to-gray eyebrows rose.

"I'll split it with you if it works out that way. That way you won't have to cut up that load of firewood."

"Huh," Seagull said. "That's mighty fine of you, sir. All the same, I should probably do the firewood job regardless. I'm getting fat."

"Getting?" Davecki asked, picking up another plate.

Seagull shoved Davecki enough to make him stagger backwards. "You take care of the watch…for now. I'll take care of the muskie. I'll take it to Lundy for mounting…now that we're rich."

"It's probably fake," Davecki said. He rehung the towel, headed for his jacket.

Seagull watched Davecki struggle into his stiff and heavy Carhartt, followed him toward the door. "I know you. You're going to snoop around and ask stupid questions. Get something simple all messed up. We should sell the watch and split the take. But no, you've got to *investigate*."

"You've got yourself a bad case of negativity, Seagull my friend. I'm not going to screw this up. It's a simple cold case, if you'll pardon the pun. In a month's time we'll both be rich."

"Believe it when I see it. I'm still cutting up your wood," Seagull said as they left the satellite station without turning out the lights.

CHAPTER 6

The Corregidor Trail, being the old Great Northern railroad grade, pals along with Federal Highway 2 from "Siberia," Wisconsin, to "Ashcan" and then "Pig Iron" just across the Michigan border. In winter, snowmobilers, most traveling faster than the cars on the highway, blow through stop signs at road crossings and have all their fun skedaddling from dive bar to dive bar. Davecki, motoring homeward to the west on the highway, noticed the slow-moving red flashing strobe light coming into and going out of view through the trees.

"That's no snowmobile," he mumbled.

Checking the temperature showing on the dashboard thermometer, "17 below," he mumbled. Mumbling being a prime feature of old age and much solitude.

Through the trees devoid of foliage, the small flashing red light was not a Crick Dick on his Skandic. The flashing was too weak and too slow. A broken snowmobile taillight? "What the heck is that?"

Davecki rounded Powder Keg corner, the spot where, in 1910, blacksmith Anvil Jarvi was heading back to his Palo farm in his brand-new Model T truck. Loaded with supplies bought at the Iron Creek Co-op, including a box of dynamite for clearing stumps, a nasty bump in the rut-filled excuse of a road set off the dynamite, destroying the newfangled Model T and, by the by, vaporizing the majority of poor Anvil in the process.

At Hollandaise Road, Davecki pointed the truck's headlights into the dark of the north toward Palo. Just as the Corregidor Trail's road crossing came into the purview of the truck's non-halogen headlights, a big dog with black and white fur that circled its chest like a girdle ran across the road a hundred feet in front of the bumper. Davecki slammed on the brakes, skidding to a stop inches from the rest of the dog team following its leader…all without a musher attached.

"Oh oh," Davecki muttered.

He jerked the 4x4 lever into four high, jammed the pickup into reverse and put the pedal to the metal. The truck leaped backwards like a bucking O. J. Bronco, er…F-150. Davecki eyeballed the outside rearview mirror like an eagle, guiding the truck backwards by the backup lights reflecting off the snowbank. In an instant he slammed on the brakes and spun the steering wheel right like a pinwheel in high wind. The truck did the sweetest reverse power slide you ever did see. While the truck was still skidding south he reefed the gear shifter to drive and floored the truck again. It was no Dodge Squad, but the four-barrel 351 Windsor under the hood responded by hurtling the truck back the way they'd come as if there was a sauna fire and the VFD needed manning in a hurry.

Half a mile later, going about 80 mph on the Town of Vern's plowed road that looked more like a landing strip, the rapidly approaching intersection of Old Highway 2 and Hollandaise presented Davecki with another challenge. A hundred feet or so to the intersection, he hammered the brakes and spun the steering wheel left in a full-lock counter-steer.

It was a beautiful thing.

The skidding arc spewed snow and ice from the truck tires. The rest of the truck followed the tires and careened around the 90-degree corner like Wayne Gretzky carving up an NHL rink. Bouncing with a bang against Rhoweder's opposite snowbank, F-150 made like Horace Greeley and headed west.

"Still got it," he mumbled to the dark windshield. Studded tires would be even faster, he thought.

The race to the next road crossing was on. Three hundred horses against, what? Ten dogs? He hadn't had the time to count as the team careened past, but he figured there were at least a dozen pups on the mainline.

Where's the musher, he wondered as the horses did their thing.

At the next trail / road crossing, Davecki slammed on the brakes again, skidding to a stop. He steered the 150 from the town road on to the snowmobile trail and leapt from the cab. Racing down the trail in the glow of the headlights, he positioned himself in the middle of the trail.

One thing about dog teams passing in the night, they are stealthy.

One minute you're standing in reflected headlight beams glowing off white snow. The next, a ghost team appears. Big Lead Dog, tongue lolling out like a long pink flag, dodges right, ignoring Silly Hooman waving arms and standing in the way. Behind Big Lead Dog, swing dogs and team dogs. Then wheel dogs. Then sled. All running silent, running deep.

"Stop! Stop!" Davecki hollered as the team flowed past like a river of black and white fur undulating along the snow packed trail. They're not stopping, he realized and, as the sled came alongside, he dove for it.

"Arrgh! Ouff!" he huffed as he landed on the basket rails.

"Whoa! Whoa!" he hollered as the sled tipped over. Merrily

they bounced along, bounced along…my fair detective!

Davecki grabbed for the bow handle as he and the sled attempted to part ways. Fumbling the grab, he did a triple salchow worthy of Nancy Kerrigan…before the knee of course…and missed.

Spinning through the dark air, he hollered, "Whoa! Whoa!" maybe more for himself than the dogs.

One thing about a Flying Wallenda ex-detective crash landing behind a dog sled, he'll grasp at any straw. Or, if he hears and feels a rope humming beneath him, a clever ex-detective intent on stopping the team in question will grab on and hold on for dear life.

Meanwhile, Clever Lead Dog with the black girdle, approaching a fat F-150 squatting in the trail squirts the blocking truck, leading the team past without hesitation.

It's one thing for a dog team to dodge a Ford. A sled? Another thing altogether. The sled bounced off the chrome bumper and caromed into the snowbank. The ricochet banged the sled into the side of the truck. Davecki, clinging to the rope with his mittened hands, rolled right at the last second to avoid being peeled off by the truck's tire.

If an ex-detective attempting to be the hero of the night is extra lucky, there is a big knot at the end of his rope. Davecki came to the end of his rope at the same time he banged into the truck's rear tire and bounced into the snowbank while being dragged along like a fat old flopping toboggan.

Another fine mess I've gotten me into, Davecki thought as the dogs dragged him toward Montana. Well, maybe North Dakota. Or Dull-uth.

Bouncing along in the dark on his belly, sputtering snow, Davecki thought, this is ridiculous. Something has to be done. He pirouetted to his butt yelling, "WHOA! WHOA! WHOA!"

There's something about a lead dog. There's no stop in the best ones. They're built from the soul outward to the mighty muscles of their hind haunches to run-run-run like there's no tomorrow. This one was good, real good.

Davecki, getting his answer, realized that the instant addition of 185 pounds, plus 20 for clothing, and boots, and the snow packed down the front of his Carhartt, wasn't deterring forward progress in any significant way. Taking a page from his youth water skiing on Cisco Whit Lake. He pulled on the rope, planted his boots and transmogrified from butt dragging to boot skiing. Skidding along like Shaun White on a snowboard, Davecki pulled himself forward one painful arm's length at a time toward the sled that had righted itself in the fashion of empty sleds bouncing along behind a running team. The flashing red light of the little battery-powered beacon on the back of the sled winked at him. I'm going to be so sore in the morning, he thought.

Too much thinking, he thought as his skiing boots inched up between the bouncing runners. Skidding along in his big boots, he lifted his toes enough to reach over the top of the skidding sled runners. Prying toes downward his weight transferred to the sled and, *voila*, instant musher again.

He grabbed the bow, dropped the drag line and stepped on the flapping section of old snowmobile track that was the snow brake.

Sweet, he thought.

Then he thought. Slower now, but still they're not stopping. Now what?

Looking to his toes he saw the silvery sheen of an aluminum foot brake with carbide spikes. He stepped on the brake. Up from the brake such a clatter arose. Little sparks flew when the carbide tips hit tiny rocks embedded in the snow. Mini geysers of snow, ice, and rocks spewed up from the brake. Standing on the brake with both feet he felt the thump, thump, thump of the brake shaking his legs at about 4.5 on the Richter Scale. He yelled, "Whoa! Whoa!" Then realized, insanity is doing the same thing over and over again and expecting different results.

Abandoning whoa he tried, "HALT! HALT! HALT!"

Nothing.

"CEASE AND DESIST!"

Run, run, run, the team answered.

Davecki got off the brake to give his rubber-band legs a break. Looking at the somber and silent trees flowing past on both sides like a tall river of silent sentinels, he realized, this is kinda neat.

"PAUSE, TERMINATE, CONCLUDE," he yelled.

Stepping back on the brake, he yelled, "STOP! DANG IT!"

Like magic, the entire team came to a stop.

Ten dogs looked back to see what the problem was.

"Good dogs!" Davecki said.

Like magic again, the team agreed and half of them laid down for a rest.

"Huh. Cool."

Now what? Davecki wondered. He looked back east down the trail. In the distance, about a quarter mile away, the red glow of burning taillights from the distant truck.

"Okay, boys and girls," he announced, "Let's see if we can find your musher."

Turning ten furry critters around in the confined space of a narrow trail just wide enough for two snowmobiles is a tangled mess of confused dogs trying their best to understand what in the world is going on. Dogs are straight-line types, sort of OCD in that regard. They don't like corners and turns for the most part. Complete 180s? Real disregard for 180s.

But, with some begging, lifting and dragging, a ten-dog-180 is doable. Though un-pretty and fraught with frustration.

With the team straightened out toward the east, Davecki yelled, "Mush!"

Lead Dog was curled around itself licking its privates. He paused grooming long enough to give Davecki a bored stare.

"Hike!" he tried.

Still with the stare. Other dogs along the line looked back.

"Don't look at me!" Davecki blurted. "Tell your leader it's time to go."

At "go" the entire team turned into all go and Davecki almost lost his grip on the bow as the sled leaped out and away. Clinging with both hands, he windmilled his big boots as fast as he could and jumped on the runners.

Huffing like a winded Shetland at the county fair horse races, Davecki pondered the heart pounding in his chest. The thumping there beat in rhythm with the scraping and thumping of the sled runners on the frozen snow. Cool, Davecki thought, watching ten dogs undulating in a line toward the future. Big Lead Dog dodged the Ford. Davecki ducked, missing the idling F-150's outside rearview mirror. No crash this time.

The deeper into the woods, the farther down the trail, the more magical the moments became. Davecki's breathing slowed. His heart eschewed an attack. The hum of sled runners on snow hypnotized. The tall balsam trees pointed their black cones to a lighter shade of sky. The taller hardwood trees scratched the sky above the pines with gnarled fingers. The silent forest slid past, mute monitors of ageless time. The undulations of dog backs reaching into the darkness ahead made him realize what the big deal was about mushing dogs. The core instinct of a human heart is to love the core instincts of dogs pulling.

A few more minutes of magic revealed a bouncing headlamp down the distant trail. Lead Dog, whatever his or her name was, barked once and made a command decision. He or she ran up to the headlamp and stopped.

Out of the gloom ahead, Davecki heard a woman's voice, "Oh, my gosh!"

Davecki went toward the light.

"Rampart! Good boy, Rampart," Woman's voice came to him as the dog licked her lips and nose.

Ugh, Davecki thought, mind flashing on what that tongue had recently been cleaning.

Looking up at Davecki, the voice asked from inside a parka hood, "How did you get them stopped and turned around?"

"Howdy, ma'am," Davecki said, trying to imitate Cousin Longmire's best western-hero drawl. The only thing missing was the clang of silver spurs. Oh, and a dose of reality.

Said woman pulled her hood back, said, "Oh my, my. Who are you and how did you get my team stopped?"

"Dave Davecki at your service, ma'am."

"I didn't think I'd see them until morning somewhere out near Burrmidji."

"Caught up with them over by Hollandaise Road."

"Were they stopped? They usually don't stop for miles and miles," the woman said. She wore a black rip-stop parka with shards of white poking out of the various rips and tears in the arms and elbows that looked like cotton balls clinging to their stems in the fall before combining. So much for stopping rips, Davecki thought. Multi-patched snow pant legs fell below the parka hem. The right leg had a big gray patch about 18 inches long. The left leg had a football shaped patch of blue denim. She should've bought Carhartts, Davecki thought. Below the patches, two fat blobs of white Air Force bunny boots.

"Oh, thank you, sir. Thank you."

The radiant glow of the lady's headlamp illuminated a round face and cheeks rosy from the cold. The rim of the parka's fur ruff resting on her shoulders sparkled with hoarfrost condensed from her breath. Her eyes, watery from the cold and wind, were blue as Lake Superior's deepest water.

"Twarn't nothing, ma'am," Davecki said. He cast what he hoped was a meaningful look up at the ghostly treetops, was that the sound of distant drums far away, far away? The haunting strum of a mellow guitar and the *Sons of the Pioneers* singing *Tumbling Tumbleweeds* in the background? Thank you, Jim Reeves.

Woman said, "Oh yes, it was. Whatever you did, it wasn't easy. That I know."

"If you say so, ma'am."

"Umm. Umm," she said. "Would you mind not calling me ma'am? Makes me feel old."

"Anything you say…umm…"

"Oh. Kaylee," she said as she raised her elbow in the Covid salute. "Kaylee Remington."

"Nice to meet you, Kaylee," Davecki said, bumping her elbow.

Remington bent and cupped Big Lead Dog's face in mittened hands, said, "Stay, Rampart! Stay!" She let go of the dog and hustled back along the string of dogs, greeting and praising each as she went. "Good dog, Rosie. Good Dog. Remmy, who's a good boy? You are. Regal, good boy. Rivka, good girl."

At the sled, she fished in the sled bag and pulled out a nasty looking steel hook-like-affair attached to a rope, threw it down to the snow and stomped on it, forcing the tines into the snow and ice.

"Wow," Davecki said. "Had I known about that I could have used it."

"Snow hook," Remington said.

"I tried to grab the sled as they went by and missed. But managed to catch the rope strung out behind."

The young woman grinned and looked down. "Yeah, that's my dragline. Sometimes I fall asleep and fall off the runners. Or the ride gets rough and I can't hold on. It's a little embarrassing, but I trail a rope to grab if I fall off. Just in case. It didn't work tonight. Though I'm glad it worked for you. Thanks again so much for helping."

Gosh. Darn. Shucks, Davecki thought, but said, "My truck's still running on the side of the trail back by Old Highway 2. I should get back to it before some meth heads come along and steal it."

"Sure thing. This has got to be good training for the Iditarod." Remington went back to Big Lead Dog, touched the black nose and said, "Good dog, Rampart. Good dog."

Rampart wagged his tail. His butt wiggled. His girdled chest shook. His black and white face smiled. One of his eyes was bright blue, the other brown.

"You're a good girl, Rhubarby girl," she said to the next dog in line as she doubled the team back the way they'd just come.

"The Iditarod?" Davecki asked. He stood back as the team executed a precision about face, far more organized than the one he'd done. "That's a big deal."

"By the yard, it's hard. By the inch, it's a cinch," she said. "One of my distant relatives helped start the race."

"Wow. Cool," Davecki said.

"Line-out. Line-out," Kaylee said, greeting and reaching out to each as the team U-turned.

"Reggie boy. You're a good boy. You too Radar. René...you so sweet. Robbie...good girl."

Davecki grabbed the sled by the bow as it scraped around on runners plowing up a neat and tidy line of snow. The 180 was no big deal with Alpha Dog Remington in charge.

The trip back to the F-150 was not as magical. Sitting in the sled bag was no fun. The jolting, the bouncing, the organ-mashing bumps made his liver quiver and his bladder not gladder. Should've walked, he thought.

It was a great relief to see the glow of the truck's headlights and a huge relief to watch Kaylee glide off into her future. "More huger" was Davecki's relief as he made yellow holes in the snowbank, anticipating firing up the sauna and getting his bruised and battered old carcass some serious heat treatment. What's that? He cocked his head and listened.

"Who cooks for you? Who cooks for you too?" he heard the barred owl call.

Another miracle of life in northern Wisconsin in December, he thought. He shut the F-150 down. Looking up at the black and silent sky with stars so close they seemed touchable, the owl called again, "Who cooks for you? Who cooks for you too?"

Neat, he thought. Very cool.

In the distance, a quarter mile or so away, a response, "Who cooks for you? Who cooks for you too?"

Behind to the south, a coyote joined the conversation, "Yip-yip-yip, oooowoo! Yip-yip-yip, oooowooo!"

Neat, Davecki thought. They're hunting together. "Whoo, whoo, whoo-whoo," He added to the chatter.

The owl nearest replied, "Who cooks for you? Who cooks for you too."

"I cook for me. I cook for me, me," he said, looking up to the treetops. I wonder where that owl is hiding. He scanned the witch-finger limbs.

Coyote called, "Yip-yip-yippy-yip."

He sounds closer, Davecki thought.

Then a different coyote voice in the distance responded, "Yip-py-yip. Yippy-yip, o-youooo!"

Movement above. What had been just a blob of black in a tree-top swelled. Wings appeared. The blob became an owl stooping, gliding on noiseless wings toward the coyote sounds.

So cool, Davecki thought, watching the owl head south to see what coyote had found. As the bird cut through the biting air, slicing the night like a knife, Davecki felt tired. Getting late, he thought. Raising his wrist to peel back his Carhartt sleeve, his gut twisted. The Rolex was gone.

CHAPTER 7

The pitiful sight of a grown man on the Corregidor Trail on hands and knees crawling around like an old pulp cutter on a week-long drunk lasted too long. It had already been a long night on the longest night of the year. Davecki gave up, drove home, went sauna, and fell into bed. Recurrent remonstrations for losing the watch precluded sleep.

It was a fake, he consoled himself. I'll find it in the morning. Or in the spring. It survived the muskie licking and kept on ticking, it'll survive a winter buried in snow along the trail. Willie Scott will groom the trail and bury it good so nobody else will find it. Why can't I fall asleep? I wonder if that Remington girl's team is any good. The Iditarod is big time. Kinda weird bumping into her out there in the middle of nowhere. You really are a doofus, losing that watch. John Wayne Carczak must have made a serious bundle of money. Carczak lost his watch, so I'm in good company I guess. Maybe it was stolen. Like Sulu's truck. I wonder what happened in Alaska when he went back. I hope nobody finds it before I get back to the trail. It's a fake. Carczak bought it from a street hustler in Seattle I bet. Carczak Gold. Survive the cold. This is getting old.

Davecki rolled over in bed, plucked the devil's tool from the nightstand. The glow of the phone's screen highlighted his angular face. The Hayfield County website page showed the GIS map of county properties. Search tool. Carczak. Davecki tapped and double tapped on the map until the property in question enlarged enough to show the boundaries of a Pesthouse Lake shoreline property.

Squinting, he mumbled, "No good."

He got up. Grabbing the sweater hanging from the doorknob, he tossed the phone back onto Aunt Brenda's bundled up quilt atop the messy bed. He stuck his toes into fleece slippers and headed for the laptop. Hovering the cursor over the property, the popup window displayed: Molly Carczak, 10251 Jackpot Lane. He opened a new window. Google Earth. Zoom. Zoom. Zoom. Maybe I should buy a Mazda. Crazy how commercials stick in your head.

"Hmm," he muttered. Click, click, click.

The screen showed an expansive array of roofs and the trails leading to the lake's remote shore, complete with boathouse that probably broke numerous DNR wetland regulations and county setback rules. He dragged the satellite view around the entire shoreline. No other houses. A private lake? Makes sense considering the name.

"Pretty fancy," Davecki muttered. Closing the windows, including the one about the difference between pawning and selling personal property at pawn shops, he shut the laptop down. He moved the machine to the chairside table. "Oh well," he said heading to bed. Move the phone. Crawl in, pull covers. Heavy sigh. Okay. "A," he said. Lord help Andy with that brain bleed. B, he thought. Lord, bless Barbara and help her son Ben with his psychotic break. C, Lord, give Carl the courage to know the difference. D, Lord, keep Davina healthy in Africa. E, Lord, bless Ernie and his kid. F, Frank, God, protect Frank stationed in Syria. By the time he got to Pete in Alaska, sleep overpowered prayer.

Disjointed dreams of hanging from the minute hand of Big Ben in London, getting swallowed into the belly of the giant fiberglass muskie in Hayward, and something about a blizzard, accompanied something resembling sleep.

The next morning a sliced banana coated with neither grapes nor nuts and smothered with applesauce, supplemented with beverage of choice, green tea, combined with the knife-edged urge to find a two-million-dollar watch pushed him out the trailer door well before dawn. The breakfast of not-champions helped reduce the slap-in-the-cheeks-shock of fifteen-below morning air. Revived by the cold, Davecki punished the F-150 at speed back to the scene of the not-crime to search for his lost big payday. The brisk walk along the Corregidor trail, watery eyes following every sweep of the bright headlamp flashing against the bright snow, each empty step eroding hope. After a lifetime of ribbing his Finnish friends with Toivo and Eino jokes, it was strange to learn that Toivo is Finnish for hope, he reflected as he scanned and rescanned the snow for any hint of gold gleaming in the headlight beam.

Mornings in Wisconsin in December are dark affairs. Lord help me find it, he prayed as his boots squeaked the crunchy snow. I wonder what the Eskimo word for squeaky snow is, he wondered. The headlamp light danced as he walked.

Two million bucks. What an idiot. Please let it be fake. No. Let it be real and let me find it and make Seagull rich. Oh, and me too. Davecki raised his head at the sound of an approaching snowmobile. The dim light of the sun's rising tinted the black sky in the east a bit bluer. Below the treetop-lined horizon, the bouncing headlight of a snowmobile approached.

Geez, those things are noisy, he thought as the engine sound changed. At least it's slowing down a little, Davecki thought as he stepped to the edge of the trail. The headlight transmogrified into a black Arctic Cat snowmobile. The operator wore a pink snowsuit topped with a white helmet. Said operator smacked the kill button down, pulled off gloves, pulled off said helmet and Davecki, keen grasper of the obvious, concluded that said operator was a woman when the cascade of long blondish hair fell like there was a film crew nearby recording a shampoo commercial.

"Dave! What the heck you doing out here this early? And on foot!"

"Hi Gayle. I lost my watch here last night. I'm looking for it."

"Oh, you mean this?" Gayle asked. She fished the Rolex out of her snowsuit pocket.

"Man! I mean, woman! God really knows how to answer prayers," Davecki yelped as she handed the watch over.

"Oh, how nice. I'm an answer to prayer first thing in the morning," Johanison said.

If you only knew, Davecki thought.

"Pretty nice watch."

"Yeah, I'm really glad you came along. What you doing out here this early?"

"Oh, just cruising around, answering prayers and running to Iron Creek to get bread crusts from Lena's bakery. I'm making a casserole for pot blessing lunch at church Sunday. I came across Old Highway 2 and my headlight reflected off something shiny so I stopped and found it."

"Your car broke down?"

"Cars are no fun," Gayle grinned. She patted the windshield of the machine, said, "Well, gotta go." She popped the kill button up, put her helmet and gloves back on, yanked the pull cord once, and zoomed away.

"Lucky dog, lucky dog, lucky dog," he muttered the refrain from the commercial as he got in and slammed the door on his suspension of disbelief.

I wonder what the next miracle is going to be, he wondered

as he cranked the heater fan to hotter than August in Texas. Turning on the overhead light, he studied the watch as the heat battled the cold. This thing has been through the mill, he realized, shaking some ice crystals from the band. The sweep hand nicked forward as if it had not a care in the world. Nor did the watch seem to be troubled over its recent traumas. Looking at the truck's dashboard clock, he realized the time was correct. For two million dollars, you'd think they could have put a date window in the thing, he thought. He de-gloved, watched-up, re-gloved, found drive and headed for town, wondering if he should stick with oatmeal at Gabe's or splurge and have two eggs and muffin toast. Maybe even hash browns. After all, I'm a millionaire now, he admitted. No bacon though. Wanna live long enough to enjoy my newfound wealth. On the other hand, I can now afford bypass surgery.

He wiggled his left hand and forearm. Made the watch do a little dance on his wrist. Feels pretty good, he thought. Maybe I'll just keep it. I'm the one who caught it. Seagull can catch his own fortune. Guy fishes enough.

Now Dave, you promised.

That promise was given in haste. It's my word against Seagull's.

But Seagull's out of work.

I'll give him a helper's fee. Finders keepers. Helpers weepers.

You're the loser if you don't share.

Okay. Okay. Geez, he thought as the yellow glow of the bright lights within Gabe's restaurant came into view.

"Your headlamp's still on, Dave," Carson said, as she plunked a cup of coffee down before Davecki took his usual seat in the corner.

"Uh, thanks, Carson," he answered, reaching up and clicking the headlamp's single action button. The light went to flash mode as Davecki fumbled to click it again. Failing to click again, he resorted to taking the headlamp and stocking cap off to get at the clicker button and shut 'er down. In doing so, his Carhartt jacket sleeve pulled back, revealing the watch.

"Wow, pretty fancy watch, Dave," Carson said. "The usual? I saw your truck coming in and told Queenie to get your oatmeal ready."

There goes my urge to splurge, Davecki thought, missing the eggs and muffin toast already. "Okay. Thanks, Carson." As Carson headed toward the kitchen, he considered saying, "Side order of bacon," but didn't want to get too crazy.

"What you up so early for? I thought you were retired," Carson said. She plunked down the bowl of oatmeal.

"More like just tired," Davecki said, picking up the tiny silver milk pitcher. "I'm going to visit the vet."

"You have a dog?"

Davecki grinned, "Not yet. Thinking about getting one."

"You need a dog, Dave."

"Maybe. We'll see."

CHAPTER 8

The saying, "It's darkest just before dawn," seems more true in wooded northern Wisconsin in December. Towering, often snow-clad, trees crowding the narrow roads keep the searching sunlight at bay longer than in the open fields of farm country down south. Dawn's delay is heightened when thick gray clouds plod past on their forced march from North Dakota to their ultimate losing battle with the Great Lakes and eastern seaboard.

The same is true of temperatures. It also gets coldest just before dawn. The temperature readout on the 150 dash reported 17 below. In the spots where Highway 97 crossed bogs and swamps, mini-clouds of misty frost floated like wandering ghosts above the tall snow banks County Plowman Rhoweder pushed up all along the Watchtower way.

Misty Frost would make a good name for someone, Davecki thought.

Wait a minute.

What was that?

Touching the brakes gently to avoid a spin-out on the frost covered road, he slowed and put the shifter into reverse. The rear tires spun on the slick surface at first, but, slowly, the truck inched backward. He turned the truck in an arc directing the headlight beams across the snowbank.

Across the ditch, a sign. Not a sign from heaven like the watch continually returning, but a bump in the snow with little towering-tilting caps of built-up snow on top of the thick cedar posts holding the half-buried sign erect despite the snow's relentless pressure. The deep drift in front of the sign curved its parabola high on both ends of the sign. In the middle, *OVE V* in nine-inch tall letters showed. This must be it, Davecki thought. He honked the horn hoping the sound waves would dislodge the snow and reveal what the rest of the sign said.

No go.

He got out, went to the side of the road, picked up a frozen chunk of snow the size of a softball that had tumbled down from the plowed-up bank and threw it at the sign.

"Clunk," the chunk clunked, bouncing off the sign. Cascading snow parted like the Red Sea to reveal the rest of the story. I'm Charlton Heston and Paul Harvey all wrapped up in one, Davecki mused.

LOVE VETERINARY. Dog, cat, cow, and horse silhouettes marked the sign's four corners. Centered at the bottom: CATHERINE LOVE DVM. Below, a Redpaw logo.

Heading south on the Town of Lowland road, the snowbanks were even higher than the main highway. Narrow was the way leading to the Carczak driveway that was fronted by an oversized mailbox. Hanging on each side of the mailbox-like saddlebags were two oversized plywood cutouts of a handsome Alaskan husky. Davecki wondered, does that violate postal regulations? The driveway was flanked by tall white pines that were either too small or simply missed the cut back in 1901 when Frederick Weyerhaeuser, that scion of ecological concern and devotee of the public interest, sent scads of desperate immigrant men with sharp axes and long misery whips into the woods to wipe out the white pine.

Curving into the circular drive made small by the encroaching snow, Davecki's approach prompted a long-legged dog to leap off the wide porch situated under a twin-gabled roof. This one was white with brown spots and long fur that looked more like unkempt hair. Shouldn't it be a husky, Davecki wondered. Maybe some sort of wolfhound-greyhound mix. As the lanky dog ran barking towards the approaching F-150, the big coral door in the middle of the porch opened. A short woman appeared and seemed to be yelling at the dog. Waving her arms, she looked cartoonish, arms all a-flutter.

The dog ignored her, kept running to the truck.

Davecki put the truck in park and popped the door, wondering if the dog was friendly. The cold air smacked his face again, accompanied by another slap, this one to his ears. The cacophony of many dogs barking punched his eardrums. Man, that's loud, he thought. Could be a nifty Native American name, he thought, Many Dogs Barking. Or Man Cloud Loud.

He glanced at the dashboard thermometer before shutting the truck down. Minus 22. He looked at the eastern sky. The fringe of trees pointed to the growing light, confirming that it was coldest just before dawn. The wiry-haired dog had circled the truck, probably peed on three tires, and appeared in the open doorway. It jumped up, planting two big white hairy paws on Davecki's left thigh.

Man, those dogs are loud, he thought again, looking past the garage where the uproar originated. Hush you muskies, he dyslexified. I wonder why God sacrificed a giant muskie to bring this watch to me?

The wire-haired hound woofed.

"Not paying sufficient attention to you, hey fella? Who's a good boy," he said, scratching behind the scraggly head. The dog leaned hard into Davecki's ministrations. "You like that, huh?"

"Get back," he said, swinging out of the truck. A big garage with two rows of concrete foundation blocks around the perimeter hunkered down under two feet of snow on its roof. I wonder if there's an Eskimo word for snow on a roof, he wondered. Two double roll-up garage doors painted coral like the house door stared unblinking like big bloodshot eyes in the middle of the half-log, deep brown siding. Beside the garage sat an older model Polaris snowmobile. Beyond the sled, an enclosure of fifty feet of chain link fence six-feet high.

Inside the fence, a husky-type dog, its front paws up on the fence, barked staccato barks at the newcomer. Puffs of white condensed dog breath puffed out of the snout at each bark. Behind the cooped-up husky, the yips and yelps and howls of a bunch more dogs lunged around the garage's corner. The jabberwocky from behind the building sounded like a pack of young wolves at the den chanting at a full moon.

To the right of the garage/kennel building, lay a low-slung house with two-foot eaves. Its roof looked strong, supported at the corners by 20-inch thick white pine uprights. This roof had maybe three feet of snow atop. Decent insulation there, Davecki thought. Behind the pine, the wide windows in the house wall glowed dim yellow.

The short woman left the porch, walked around the corner of a snow-covered red Dodge Dually that had a big red and black box van on its back. Snow obscured all the letters except IAN. Veterinarian, no doubt, Davecki thought. Looks like an old retired ambulance, he thought again. To the left of the van, the barking dog inside its chain link enclosure had jumped down and was running forth and back along its prison wall.

The lady of the porch approached. "Myles! Heel!" she said.

Myles ignored her and continued snuffing Davecki's crotch.

Pushing Myles away, Davecki looked at the lady.

"Fancy meeting you again so soon," Kaylee Remington said.

"Kaylee! You look different without the parka."

"No kidding. What can I do for you?" She looked over at the dog pen where the doggy symphony continued unabated. "Rosie! Shut it!" she yelled.

The dog in the front pen quit pacing, stopped barking, plunked its haunches down and glared through the fence.

"Good dog!" she yelled.

The dog, in Davecki's estimation, didn't look all that pleased. More of a "You really know how to ruin a party, lady," look on her pretty face. Behind the dog named Rosie, the canine orchestration may have subsided a little, but just.

"So, what's up?" Kaylee asked.

"I'm wondering if Molly Carczak might be available," Davecki answered.

The ruddy-from-the-cold skin of Remington's round face blanched. Her deep blue eyes hardened. She said, "Grandma Molly passed away three weeks ago."

The chill of the frozen morning was warm compared to the frigid crawl of icy regret Davecki felt in the small of his back. "I'm so sorry, ma'am," he said, looking down.

"There you go with the ma'am thing," Kaylee said.

"Sorry. Sorry."

She opened her mouth to speak when the dogs behind the garage erupted in an even more intense uproar. A flash of gratitude blew across Kaylee's face like a quick wind. She turned on her heel and sprinted toward the dog enclosure.

What now, Davecki asked himself. Call it a day, get in the truck, beat feet, and forget the whole thing? He wiggled the meal-ticket watch on his wrist. Its weight felt like a gravity well...if that's the term, he thought. More like a black hole of gold and fears and greed drawing him into the unknown. The woman's yelling and the dog pack's barking and yipping magnetized the watch, or Davecki himself, the commotion drawing him toward the subtle attraction of chaos.

Around the corner there was a second chain link dog pen as wide as the garage wall. Remington stood in the middle of a cascade of undulating canines that resembled Hall Rapids on the Brule. She was being, to put it delicately…firm. Yelling names and commands. "Rembrandt! NO! Rambo! NO! Roberta! NO!" The dogs in the fight didn't seem to notice when she grabbed a handful or two of hide and hair and tossed a given animal aside. The dogs Remington sent flying took to their new trajectories without complaint. As soon as said flying dog landed on solid ground, it surged like water back to the melee.

"Wow," Davecki muttered from outside the fence.

"Don't just stand there! Help!" Remington barked.

The embarrassment from moments ago resurfaced to a smaller degree and motivated the casual observer. Davecki lifted the gate latch and stepped way out of his comfort zone.

Remington picked up a whitish, brownish, blackish, dog with a ring of white fur circling its neck and flung the creature at Davecki. The flying Wallenda struck him in the chest. He clamped around the dog's belly and chest with both arms.

"That's Randy! Box him!" Remington yelled.

"Rivka!" Remington cried. "You're in heat!"

That explains a thing or two, Davecki thought.

"Stuff him in his box, idiot!"

Davecki, holding the squirming, barking dog, followed Remington's look to the side of the garage where a rank of wooden doors ran along the wall. Each box had a foot-square door with holes in it mimicking a dog paw. Above each door, a name. Espying RANDY hand painted in white, Davecki filed a flight plan, saying, "Here we go, fella."

Randy got with the program. He settled down a bit, which was good, as Davecki grabbed the rope stretching upward from the door to a hole in the roof soffit above. The dog knew the drill. As Davecki slid the door up, Randy clawed his way into the box, kicking straw out as he entered.

As Davecki let go, the door slid down into place. Davecki turned and, like Willy Mays at the warning strip, snagged another flying dog launched from Remington's toss.

"Rembrandt," she hollered.

As Rembrandt bounced off Davecki's chest, the formerly-known-as-an-artist-dog swung its gleaming choppers around and bit down hard on Davecki's arm. One nice thing about thick Carhartt winter coats, they're fang-proof for the most part.

"Geez. Lighten up, Remmy," Davecki said, as he mushed over to the artist's box. This name was painted with Michelangelo-red paint.

Rembrandt, having eschewed biting for barking and squirming, came to Jesus when he-she-it, like Rampart, came to understand it was being boxed. "In you go!" Davecki huffed as he nose-dived the whirling dervish dog into its box.

The door fell into place, the attached rope snapping straight. Remington arrived with another air-clawing canine hugged to her chest.

"Rene!" she yelped.

The next door was Rene's. Davecki lifted the sliding door. Remington heaved the dog in. "Rene! You bad dog!" she said.

Meanwhile, the dogfight at the O.K. Kennel continued. There were still half a dozen dogs growling, snapping jaws, and barking. Davecki seized another husky.

"That's Rabble," Remington said.

Rabble in rouser box.

"Rambo," Remington repeated.

Rambo in Stallone box.

"Rollie."

Stuffing Rollie into his or her dog box, Davecki reflected, if I ever get a husky as a pet I'm naming him Rolex. He'll make an excellent watchdog.

"Thanks for your help. I need coffee." She shook her head, turned for the gate, "Care to join me?"

"A little caffeine might help just now."

Remington grabbed Rivka by the collar. "Into isolation with Rosie," she said. She clanked the gate shut behind Davecki.

Reminds me of a jail cell door closing, he reminisced.

CHAPTER 9

On the porch of the house, the hound Myles rose and turned nose toward the coral door. "Myles is very detached from the sled dogs," Remington said as she opened the door beneath the three-foot-long hand-routed wooden sign saying LOVE VETERINARY. One of the things that makes a Wisconsin winter tolerable is entering a warm building and feeling the distinctive feel and smell of wood heat. Davecki flexed his cold nose and sniffed the appealing fragrance permeating the room. The entrance was actually the gateway to a waiting room. Three metal folding chairs with padded vinyl seats and backs placed six feet apart rested comfortably beneath a REDPAW dog food sign, and a large glass box frame with at least a hundred photos of dogs, cats, llamas and other pets. A pair of bunny boots were flopped over beside one of the chairs.

"We have to go through," Remington said, tossing her jacket to the boot chair as she headed to the opposite door beyond a short counter. On top of the counter lay a short stack of Covid masks. A hand lettered table tent stood next to them: Masks are mandatory. Ninety-nine cents was the minimalist message. To the left of the doorframe a button with a sign that said, RING FOR SERVICE. This is tidy, Davecki thought, looking at the organized display rack of pet-related items for sale. Maybe even antiseptic. Or possibly OCD. Remington tossing her jacket aside as she did struck Davecki as out of character with the room's appearance.

Davecki followed suit, tossing his Carhartt at a chair. It missed and slipped to the floor, the zipper rasping across the chair seat.

The next room was an exam room with a big platform scale and a table and a wide off-white two-door cupboard above a desk with a chair tucked under. To the right, a door labeled SURGERY. Straight ahead, another door with no label.

Davecki followed Remington through the door into living quarters. On the immediate left was a small bathroom about three times larger than an airplane lav. Myles clicked toenails across the tile floor toward a room with a large couch visible and vanished around a corner. Obeying one of the three rules of manly old age: *Never Pass up a Bathroom*, Davecki asked, "May I use the restroom?"

"Of course. I'll get the coffee started."

In the wide-open kitchen, Davecki sat at a high, straight backed chair at the end of a high counter that partitioned the room from the breakfast nook that had high and wide windows on one wall. Through the windows, Old Man Winter stared, looking rather glum, Davecki thought. The living quarters bordered on chaotic, with newspapers and dirty dishes and socks and dog dishes making up the main elements of decor. Maybe not quite chaos, Davecki thought, more like lived in. Heavily lived in.

"Why did you want to talk to Grandma Molly?" Remington asked. She plunked two mugs, each with silk-screened portraits of sled dogs, on the counter. She opened the freezer, pulled out a Cameron coffee packet and tipped beans into a white plastic grinder.

"I bought a Rolex watch at an auction in Hayward," Davecki lied. Why the lie, he wondered. "The inscription on the back led me to Carczak Gold, registered in Fairbanks, which led here," he eased his conscience with a part of the truth.

Remington dribbled hot water from an electric pot onto the coffee grounds in the Chemex. The pot had more buttons on the handle than a TV remote. "Huh," Remington said, standing over the coffee, holding the kettle, studying the soaking grounds. "Molly never mentioned a Rolex. Kitty either. But then, I didn't get to spend a lot of time with Molly before she got sick. If even a little of what I've heard about Grandpa Jack is true, a Rolex wasn't beyond him."

But, two million bucks, Davecki thought. "Who's Kitty?"

Remington's eyes squinted. "Grandma and Grandpa's daughter. Kitty? You know, Catherine Love? Everyone calls her Kitty. You don't know her? I thought you were a friend of the family or something."

"No. I just came upon the Rolex and wanted to find out more." Still not telling the whole truth, huh Dave, Davecki thought.

Remington stood, pot in hand, studying Davecki. The pot trembled a little.

Davecki slid off the stool. "I apologize. I misled you. I didn't mean to. I can leave." He got off the chair and moved toward the exit.

"No. No. Sit. Sit. After last night, and the way you waded into the dog pen, I just thought you were…I don't know…familiar. Like a friend of the family or something."

"It's a bad habit I have."

"What's that?"

"Being too friendly."

"That's bad?" She nodded toward Davecki's vacated chair. "We may as well have coffee. I made too much otherwise."

"Kind of you." Davecki returned to his seat.

Without looking up from the pour-over, she said, "Seems like being friendly is a good thing."

"It is and it isn't. Lotta times people get the wrong idea. Lotta paranoia going around since Covid." Davecki scrubbed his chin. Get to the point, he thought.

"John sounds like a real character."

"John?" She finally looked at Davecki.

"You know, John Carczak. Molly's husband."

Remington smiled and chuckled. "Oh, you mean Grandpa Jack. Nobody around here calls him John. There's a lot I don't know."

"Umm. What do you know?" Davecki spun both coffee mugs on their bottoms so the handles faced opposite of each other. He pushed them toward the edge of the counter as Remington brought the pour-over to the cups and trickled the coal black liquid.

"Ha!" she said. "At last I found someone who knows less about my real family than me." She set the coffee maker aside.

Davecki looked her in the face. "I'm confused."

"So am I. You want milk in this?" She nudged the Rampart mug toward him. "I think I made it a little strong."

"It does look like tar," he said. "Yeah. I'll take some milk."

Remington went to the fridge that didn't look like a fridge. Instead of being stainless steel or enamel it was a wood paneled affair that looked like it was part of the wall. She handed Davecki a yellow half-pint carton of milk, opened a drawer, distributed two spoons. "Two years ago I decided to try and find my birth mother. Grandma Remington in Bethel encouraged me. I contacted the agency. One thing led to another and here I am."

Davecki poured milk until the black coffee took on the color of a brown chicken egg. He stirred and stirred as Remington poured and poured milk into her Rosie cup. He extracted his spoon, noting that the brew hadn't dissolved the metal.

She didn't seem to notice him wince at the coffee's strength. "Sounds like there's a lot more to it."

"No kidding. There was all kinds of paperwork and lots and lots of questions. And more paperwork. And even counseling. I quit all kinds of times. But then I'd get the bug and go at it again." She sipped her coffee. Davecki watched to see her wince from the brew's strength. His expectation was unrewarded.

"That had to be hard," he said.

"Yeah. It was. But I'm glad I did it now."

"So John, err, Jack was your Grandpa. That makes Catherine your birth mother?"

"Yup. I'm going to be a vet, just like Kitty and Molly. But first I want to run the Iditarod."

"And you're not joking when you call her Kitty?"

Remington sipped more brew. She eyed Davecki above the cup. Both Rosie and Remington studied him. "It is sort of funny, I guess. But I've hardly ever heard anyone call her Catherine. Once a guy called her Cat Love and boy, did he get an ear full."

Davecki picked up Rampart. His hand trembled as he lifted the cup. He plunked it down.

"Yeah…it's strong all right," Remington said with a grin. "Gotta be if you chase tails all night." She smirked, "Or if you're chasing after tails all night."

"So. I'm confused a little. The county records said this was Molly Carczak's place. How come it's Love Veterinary?"

Remington blinked. Rosie did not. "That much I know. Catherine Carczak married Lawrence Love. They met at the U. He was in med school. She was in vet school. They were only married a year when he went to Iraq for the war." She looked down.

"Don't tell me," Davecki said.

"Awful. His MASH unit got hit with a rocket."

More silence as the truth of that settled on the conversation. Behind Remington, across the tile floor, a mouse scurried from the corner to under the center island.

"How long ago was that?"

"I don't know. Whenever the war was."

Davecki forced another sip of the bitter brew, "Had to be horrible for her."

"Tell me about it."

More silence. No more mouse sightings. Their sad, silent contemplations were interrupted by the sound of toenails clicking on tile. Together they looked toward the sound. A big black Labrador dog with a face sporting white hair from nose to eyebrows walked stiffly toward them.

"Big Dog! You're up. Nice to see you moving around. Come to meet Mr. Davecki?" The dog's legs moved like a walking stick insect.

The old dog wagged its tail, hobbling forward. It had a huge tumor bulging from its left shoulder. Cobbler's kids got no shoes, Davecki thought.

Remington knelt, cradled Big Dog's face. Kissed his nose. Davecki dismounted and joined the affection, scratching the old Lab on the neck. Big Dog raised eyebrows and looked at the newcomer, an aura of pain shone from glaucoma-shrouded eyes.

Changing the subject, Davecki said, "So, I take it Molly gave the vet business over to Catherine?"

"Would you mind calling her Kitty? It sort of bugs me to hear her called Catherine for some reason. And, yes. Molly and Kitty practiced together until Molly retired. It wasn't long before they discovered breast cancer…." Remington went silent.

"I'm really sorry. Really, really sorry. So many bad things happening to good people," Davecki said, continually scratching Big Dog as Remington stroked the dog's backbone.

"You must be pretty special for him to get up for a meet-n-greet," she said.

"Thanks for that, Big Dog," Davecki said.

Remington stood and returned to her coffee.

Davecki too abandoned Big Dog, favoring the lure of the powerful coffee. "I'm a little unclear about the Alaskan disappearance."

"So's everybody," Remington said. "All that's known is that he went to Alaska and they found the truck and dog. Troopers up there figured he fell hiking in the mountains or a bear got him. Big Dog probably knows what happened. The Troopers found him sitting by Grandpa Jack's truck."

"When was that?"

"Not real sure about that. Like maybe ten years ago? It's hard to keep track of all the dates and stuff."

A melodious doorbell sound came out of nowhere.

"Someone's out front," Remington said. "Gotta go."

They passed Big Dog limping back to the living room as they headed out. Davecki bent to pat the old boy's head. Wish I could interview you, he thought.

CHAPTER 10

"Hard to believe one family has had so much tragedy," Stanski said. He dragged a chair out from under Davecki's round oak table. Easing himself into the chair, he slowly twisted his neck far to the right, then far to the left. "Man, my neck is tight."

"Some people's roads have more potholes than others," Davecki said. He shoved a Corelle plate piled high with fried crappie fillets in front of the anguished neck twister.

"Thanks, man."

Heading to his chair on the other side of the round table, his own plate in hand, Davecki said, "I wonder if Carczak really died up there."

Stanski masticated crappie while looking at Davecki. Swallowed. "Man this is good." He forked up another bit of fish flesh. Before inserting same, said, "How long's it been?"

"Remington said she thought it was around ten years ago. I haven't done a search yet to pinpoint a date."

"What does it matter?" Stanski asked. "You've got the watch. Don't mess up a good thing."

Davecki chewed. Looked up from his fillet. "Too late. I told Kaylee about it."

"Kaylee?"

"Kitty Love's daughter. The musher lady I helped out. Remember? You having a senior moment or something?"

"I'm not the old retired guy." Stanski eyeballed Davecki, shook his head, "I notice you're not rushing out to have the watch appraised."

"All in good time, mon frère."

Stanski turned his attention to the fish. "It might just have gotten knocked overboard or got kicked into an ice hole."

"Yeah. I hear ya. Anything's possible. Seagull and I almost lost the thing last night right after we found it."

"Huh?" Stanski sipped his tea.

"I tossed the watch to Seagull last night in the tent and it almost fell back into the lake."

"Smooth move, ex-lax."

"No kidding." Davecki stood, headed for the gas range. "More?" he asked.

"Of course," Stanski said. "You know, Dave. Seagull's probably right. You guys should just sell the thing and take the money."

"Yeah, probably. But it bugs me. Not knowing."

"Well, you didn't turn up anything with the Remington girl?"

Davecki returned with the last of the fillets. "You can't say girl anymore, Stan."

"Oh? Why's that?"

"Not sure. All I know is Davina said it's illegal these days."

"How's she doing? She like working in Africa?" Stanski forked more fish into his maw.

"She's really in her wheelhouse. Helping people. Curing people."

"But a leper colony?"

"Stan, get it right. It's a hospital where leprosy is treated. I told you before, man."

"Sorry. My bad."

"Besides," Davecki added, "there's also Ebola."

"No kidding? She's a saint, man."

"No kidding. When she found me, I found gold," Davecki said, shaking his head. "As far as Remington goes, she said that Carczak went to Alaska and vanished. They found his truck and dog but no body, no evidence of a crime, no nothing. And in ten years or so he hasn't resurfaced."

"Eventually declared dead, I suppose," Stanski said. "What about the watch?"

"I'm going back to the Carczak place this afternoon to talk to Kitty Love."

Stanski stopped his last forkful of fish halfway to his mouth. "You're kidding me. Kitty Love?"

"It's true."

"Seriously? Kitty Love?"

"Believe it, mon frère."

"Unbelievable."

"Wanna join me?"

"No. I'm going to physical therapy in Poplar. Those ladies are miracle workers." He twisted his neck some more.

"I'm telling ya, man. Get one of those My Pillows."

"Wouldn't take one if you gave it to me. That's how much I hate that commercial."

"You got a problem, Stan."

"No. You got a problem. More than one."

"Such as?"

"You got a two-million-dollar watch that probably belongs to the Carczak family and you're going to visit said family and you're going to have to return it."

"Finders keepers. Losers weepers."

"Not when it comes to two million."

"Possession is nine-tenths of the law."

"You just keep living that dream. I gotta go." Stanski scraped his chair back, burped, headed for the door. "Thanks for breakfast, man. Hit the spot."

"Thank Seagull, he gave up the fillets."

"I would if I could but I can't so I shan't," Stanski said, opening the trailer door to a strong blast of cold wind. "Man, this winter is getting old."

"Don't get your underwear in a bundle. Sinto DeMars is coming."

"Don't you mean Cinco de Mayo?" Stanski stood in the open doorway, grinning.

"No. I mean that Sinto DeMars is coming to the Oulu Cultural and Heritage Center this weekend to sing and play old Finnish tunes. Wanna go?"

"Thanks for the invite, but no. I can't stand scratchy violin."

"Cretin."

"Takes one to know one."

"Quit standing there with the door open. You born in a barn or something?"

Stanski grinned, fanned the door open wider, shuffled it forth and back pumping more cold air into Davecki's tiny home.

"I'm going to have to kill you, brother."

"Admit you're wrong. That it's Cinco de Mayo and I'll leave without a struggle."

Davecki rose from his chair, glowered at Stanski, "I'm not wrong. My cousin Sinto DeMars from Helsinki is coming to ski the Birkie which means warm weather is on the way. It always warms up for the Birkie. Now get out or get in!"

Stanski bowed slightly, stepped through the doorway, said, "Nolo Contendere to you too, hombre," and slammed said door shut.

"Thanks for help with the dishes, jerk!" Davecki yelled.

"De nada!" Stanski's hollered reply filtered through the thin aluminum wall.

CHAPTER 11

Four inches of fresh snow made the drive treacherous. There were five vehicles in the ditches between Davecki's and Kitty Love's place. He shook his left arm, felt the weight of the Rolex. I should just keep it, he thought. Hayward will start taking wood eventually and Seagull will get back on the road. Covid will get sorted out and the whole world will be comprised of masked men…and women, the Lone Ranger notwithstanding.

The long and winding road to Love's door held another surprise. As Davecki came around Winneboujou bend, he beheld flashing red lights, a tow truck and the underside of a car, wheels pointing skyward. The flashing lights belonged to Stanski's squad, the deputy standing beside it as he waved a blue Subaru past. Davecki stopped behind the squad. Stanski walked to the 150's passenger side, got in, saying, "Colder than a well digger's ass in January."

"You ever wonder how they got that saying?"

Stanski looked at Davecki, grimaced. "Not once in all my life.

But I'm about to learn. Am I right?"

"You're a lucky man, Stan. Having me for a friend."

"Right."

"The well digger's butt was always against the back wall, shoveling in a circle all the time."

"My life is forever changed," Stanski said. He looked out at the wreck in front of them.

"You got that right." Davecki looked away from the tow truck's progress righting the overturned car. "What's the story here?"

"Lady turtled her Honda. Avoiding a deer, she said. Hit the snowbank and flipped."

She should've bought a Buick, Davecki thought.

"Hang around until I clear this. I'll take you up on your offer to visit Kitty Love. I'm thinking there will be hot coffee, a treat, and inside seating. Car coming," he said as he popped the door open and slid off the seat.

Again Davecki flinched at the cold and said, "Sure," as the door slammed.

Davecki turned the radio on, listened to the propaganda for a bit, realized silence is golden and shut the noise off. Honda safely on the Vulcan tow, Stanski walked up to Davecki's window going down.

"You wanna park in the Winneboujou lot?"

"Sure."

"How'd you find out where the Carczak place is?" Stanski asked.

"If it weren't for Norvado and Google, I wouldn't know nuttin'."

Stanski studied Davecki. "You seriously think I'm not going to grab that low hanging fruit?"

"Huh?"

Stanski shook his head. "I rest my case."

The town road to the Carczak place was already plowed. "I ran a BC on Kitty Love and nothing came up. That made me curious," Stanski said.

"Huh," Davecki muttered.

"So I dug a little deeper and her real name really is Catherine Love."

"I could have told you that," Davecki answered.

"You didn't have coffee this morning, did you?" Stanski asked.

"How'd you know?"

"Just a wild guess."

As they approached the Carczak-Love driveway, an old maroon Tahoe with a Western plow pushed snow away from the husky-shrouded mailbox. The Tahoe did a whiskey turn in front of the squad and pointed back toward town. As the driver rolled past the squad, his window powered down. He stopped and said, "Doesn't look like anyone's home. But you never know. It's all plowed out now though."

"Thanks, Frosty" Stanski said as the driver rolled away.

"Many more driveways before he sleeps," Davecki quipped.

"You too funny, pal," Stanski said as he pointed the squad up the driveway.

"That looks slippy," Davecki said of the uphill grade.

"Slippy?"

"Yeah, it's Canadian for slippery. Learned that from my relleys in Toronto."

Stanski gunned the Charger. The AWD jumped up the slippy incline like a bear cub climbing a popple tree.

"Sweet traction," Davecki said.

"I can hardly believe we got along without it all these years."

The big porch had a bright light burning in the center of the high ceiling. "You take the lead," Stanski said before they got out.

On the left, the dog kennel was unusually quiet. Two dogs stood at the fence studying the interlopers. No barking now. "Remington must be on a training run," Davecki said.

On the porch, three shovels leaned against the half-log siding. Two were plastic and broken beyond use. The third aluminum scoop type was flat on its back, smeared with blood streaks glistening in the harsh light of the overhead bulb.

"Shit," Stanski said, breaking leather.

Davecki instinctively faded to the right of the porch, to the edge of the house. Peering around the corner, he signaled back to Stanski with a thumbs up.

Stanski went to the door, Glock in hand. Knocking loudly, "Sheriff!" he announced.

Should have brought my Kimber, Davecki thought as he stayed close to the wall and sidled toward the knocking Stanski.

"Sheriff!" Stanski was about to do another Glock knock when the door swung wide.

"I heard you the first time! Geez. Lighten up!" a woman's voice pushed out ahead of a silver-handled stainless-steel cart on black wheels.

Stanski stepped back and away from the onrushing cart.

"What the hell?!" the woman said. Looking at the gun, she asked, "You going to shoot me or something?!" She reached back fast to slam the door in the face of the wire-haired dog from yesterday. "Stay, Myles!" she yelled.

Stanski, dodging the cart, holstered his weapon as the speaker pushed the cart past. She was five feet tall and shrouded in a blue parka that would fit Andre the Giant. A couple hundred, or maybe twenty-five, embroidered patches covered the arms, sides, back and front of the parka, all indicating one sled dog race or another. The coyote fur ruff on the parka hood hung back from brown hair bulging out from under a black stocking cap. The cart, Davecki saw, was loaded with bloody red chunks of dark meat. That explains the bloody shovel, he thought.

"No ma'am," Stanski said, "We saw fresh blood and…."

"Like typical cops you assumed someone had been murdered, I suppose," the speaker said. She looked away from Stanski, took Davecki in and asked, "Who's your lap dog? Where's his uniform?" She continued ramming the cart across the porch.

"He's my supervisor," Stanski said.

"Baloney," the woman said. "What do you bozos want? I got dogs to feed."

So much for Stan's inside seating, coffee and a treat theory, Davecki thought. Remington was way more hospitable.

The woman zipped along the porch past Stanski, who flattened against the wall to avoid being a hit and run. Davecki picked up the aluminum scoop and leaned it against the wall with the other two shovels and skittered after the action. The blood trickled downward, making red ice trails as it descended.

"You're Catherine Love?"

"Who's asking?" She pushed the cart right to the edge of the porch. It banged hard onto the ground as the big front wheels launched into mid-air. The woman kept pushing. The cart crashed to the frozen pathway heading toward the kennel.

The two dogs in the front kennel barked and wagged their tails and butts, squirming at the sight of the steaming food cart rolling toward them.

Scooting after the departing cart, Stanski said, "Deputy Stanski, ma'am. Hayfield County."

"Who's your pal?"

Stanski and Davecki followed the fast-moving cart pusher.

"My old partner."

"Retired, ma'am," Davecki contributed. She sure seems crabby, Davecki thought. Understandable, considering she just lost her mother.

"Don't call me ma'am. What's up?" the woman asked, pushing the cart to the shoveled path along the fence. She walks like someone who's got lots to do, Davecki thought. The all-business parka wearer stopped her forward progress beside the chain link fence. She reached to the big pan of bloody meat on top of the cart, grabbed a chunk and tossed it over the top rail of the fence. The dogs attacked the snack. "Rosie! NO!" she hollered as she tossed a second snack over the fence. The other dog dove for the second helping. "There you go, Rivka," Love said.

Manna from heaven for the two dogs in heat, Davecki thought.

Love reversed direction, pulling the cart around to the rear kennel. Both men had to lean backwards to let her and the meat cart pass. Love looked Davecki directly in the eyes going by. Davecki staggered to keep from tumbling into the shoveled up snowbank. Stanski grabbed Davecki's arm.

"Thanks," he said, shaking his head at Stanski.

"She's the determined sort," Stanski stage whispered.

"No kidding," Davecki said. He recalled the look in her blue eyes, the state of her face. Chronic fatigue. Or stress, he thought as they followed the doggy meal ticket.

Love barehanded slabs of meat, flinging them over the fence into partitioned-off kennels. The hot chunks of meat slapped the frozen ground, steaming like fresh-plopped cow pies.

All along the narrow path shoveled through the deep snow, the food flew over the fence. From behind the dog box doors came whining and barking, scratching and clawing. At the end of the line, Food Flinger Lady went into reverse, pushing Stanski and Davecki back the way they'd followed.

"Beef hearts and beaver carcass," Parka Lady announced. "Pretty chewy," she explained as she took a green hand towel from a parka pocket. Wiping her hands cleaner, she extended her right hand to Stanski. "Catherine Love everybody calls me Kitty, Officer...what was it again?"

I wonder how she knows it's chewy, Davecki wondered.

"Stanski," Stanski said. "Sorry. Can't shake hands anymore. Covid-19 and all."

"Oh yeah. Forgot," Kitty Love said. "To what do I owe the dubious honor of your presence, gentlemen?" She turned toward the garage. The men followed.

Remington must not have told her about the watch, Davecki assumed.

Inside, the acrid smell of urine and poo and dusty smell of straw ruined the smell of wood heat. The concrete floor was strewn with straw from a stack of a dozen bales in the center of the car stall. Along the wall to the right, the bank of dog boxes. A lot calmer sounding than yesterday, Davecki thought.

Love shoved the cart away. It banged into two pallets of Red-paw dog food bags. She turned right and grabbed the haft of a five-foot long wooden handle with a rope threaded through about halfway from the handle to the pivot point. She grunted and heaved on the handle. The attached rope lifted all the dog box doors simultaneously.

Genius, Davecki thought.

The sound of claws scratching echoed as the canines headed for lunch.

"That'll keep 'em occupied," Kitty said. She shed her many-patch parka, trudged to a big black cast iron stove against the far wall and commenced to adding more firewood to the already burning fire in the stove.

Stanski eyeballed Davecki as Kitty did her thing on bended knee. The backside of her snow pants was split wide open.

She should've bought Carhartts, Davecki thought.

Kitty slammed the heavy firebox doors shut. She shuffled to the overstuffed chair sitting in the corner four feet away.

Pretty nice chair for a garage, Davecki thought.

Sitting on the chair's arm, she wiped her hands again on her nylon snow pants. The right knee of the pants had a big patch sewn over. "So, what's up?" She studied her visitors, her round face and brown eyes moving from man to man. "This about Dad's watch?"

Davecki felt his gut clench. So, Remington did mention it. Crunch time, he thought. Do I tell her? Show her? I lied to Remington. Truth, Dave. Truth.

Stanski gave Davecki the *busted* look.

That's what lying gets you, Davecki realized, a lot of needless anxiety.

"Yes," he said, hoping his hesitation wasn't too obvious. If it was, he'd chalk it up to Alzheimer's. He took the watch off his wrist, handed it over, asked, "Was this your father's?"

Carczak-Love took it, rolled it across her fingers, inverted the band. Studied the backside. "Yup."

Davecki thought about asking if it was a real Rolex, but, in an instant stopped himself.

She handed the watch back to Davecki.

"You don't want it?" Stanski asked.

"No. Mom bought it at an estate sale in Nome for twenty-five dollars. When Dad vanished she made her last trip to Alaska to fetch Big Dog, the pickup, and the watch that he left behind. She came to hate Alaska. Me too. She threw the watch in the lake last summer after she found out she had cancer too. That thing stands for everything up there I hate. How'd you end up with it?"

It was Davecki's turn to twist the watch between his fingers. Looking at it, he said, "Believe it or not, I caught a muskie. It was in the belly of the fish."

"If I was you, I'd throw it back in the lake. Or the dump. It's nothing but trouble. Mom actually thought it was cursed. She even said once that she thought the watch owner from Nome who died might have been a Nazi hiding out."

"Seriously?" Stanski asked.

"Who knows if she was serious? She spent enough time up there mining. Got to know the locals pretty good."

Davecki wondered. It took her ten years to throw the watch away?

Stanski said, "Well, you've got to admit it didn't bring the muskie much luck."

"Pfft," Davecki said.

Love glanced at the swivel-hip Elvis clock gyrating above the workbench. "I wonder where Kaylee is. She should be back by now."

Davecki wondered if Love knew about Remington getting separated from her sled the other night.

"You the guy who caught the team?" She looked at Davecki.

"Yup."

He wondered. I caught the team. I caught the watch. Next thing you know I'll catch Covid. Maybe I should ditch this thing.

"Thanks," Love said. "I'm a little worried about her. If you gentlemen will excuse me, I'd like to go look for her."

Davecki was tempted to ask again if she wanted the watch, but curbed his enthusiasm. "No problem," he answered.

"No problem," Stanski said.

At the door Davecki nodded at a framed 8 x10 black and white photo hanging on the wall next to the doorway. Two guys sitting on a big rock next to a stream, gold pans in hand. "That your dad?" he asked.

"Yeah. On the right. That was before he hit it big. I should throw that away too."

"Who's the other guy?" Stanski asked.

"Harry Harrison," Love answered.

Davecki thought he heard a little anxiety in her voice.

Stanski bent toward the photo squinting a little and moving forth and back to get the scene in focus.

"You mean they didn't hit it big together?" Davecki asked as Stanski studied the image.

"Long story. The mine by Fairbanks was a bust at first. Harrison ditched and then dad hit a big pay streak. He went to Nome after and did even better. I gotta get going, guys." She zipped up her parka.

Straightening his nearly six-foot frame, Stanski said, "Sorta reminds me of those old-time gold rush photos from the 1800s."

"By the time Dad was done the place looked like the moon," she said.

"What happened to Harrison?" Davecki asked.

"Got sent up, last I heard." She opened the door to Old Man Winter lurking outside like the elephant in the living room.

In the squad, rolling back down the slippy driveway, smelling the exhaust smoke of Love's Polaris sled leading them, Stanski said, "Well, now you know. The watch is a knock-off. If it was worth two-mil, she'd a kept it."

"Yeah, too bad. Or she doesn't know. It's gotta be worth something though."

"What would you do if it was worth two-mil? Keep it? Or give it back?"

"Probably have to give it back. Maybe she'd give me a finder's fee."

"You're a saint. You know that?"

"Ha! Actually, I'm feeling a little like Harrison right now."

"How's that?"

"He thought he was going to get rich. Ended up with nothing. I was hoping the watch was really worth two mil."

"Me too," Stanski said. "A three-way split would've been sweet."

CHAPTER 12

Davecki and Stanski let the silent miles back to Winneboujou roll by as each thought their ADD thoughts. I wonder if the watch is real? Even fake, it's worth something. Musta been some sorta bad stuff happened up in Alaska for Love to reject it out of hand? Good thing I don't believe in curses. I wonder if Stanski really wants some money? He was kidding, right? I wonder if I'll be able to give Seagull half. Me and my big mouth. The best thing is to keep it. Solves that problem. That poor muskie. What would Jesus do? What would Seagull do? He'd keep it, I bet.

Stanski wondered...maybe I'll stop at Cenex for free coffee and chat up that cutie with the tattoos. Nice to be a Deputy of the Law. Free brew. Half price meals. What new scheme can I cook up to torture Dave? Maybe I'll call him when he's away and say there's a fire call to his address. That his sauna is on fire. That'll rattle him. He slowed the squad at the ENTRANCE sign for the Winneboujou lot.

"You know," Davecki said. "That sign is wrong. It should say exit."

"What you talking about? It's the entrance to the parking lot."

"But it's the exit from the road."

Stanski turned off the highway. "Do you actually think this stuff up? Or are you spending too much time on the Internet?"

"Well, if you're driving down the freeway and want to get off the freeway you take the exit. If you want to get on the freeway, you use the entrance. Right?"

The newest torture came to Stanski in a flash of brilliance. He slowed the car to a crawl across the parking lot toward Davecki's F-150. "This isn't I-35 in downtown St. Paul, pal."

"Oh, you mean where Jesse Ventura said drunken Irishmen laid out the streets?"

"He said that?" Stanski asked, slowing the squad even more.

"Speed it up a little, brother, or I'm going to have to kill you."

Grinning, Stanski said. "I've just been thinking…."

"I thought I smelled smoke."

"Thanks, pal. I was just remembering. Last week getting gas at Cenex in Brule there was a guy on the other side of the pump that was a dead ringer for the guy in Love's picture, and don't tell me the dead ringer joke…again."

"You're no fun."

The Charger crept across the long narrow parking lot, grumbling like a hungry feral cat's stomach as it stalked a mouse. Stanski drummed fingers on the steering wheel. "I chatted the guy up a little. Said his name was Angelo Calisto and that he was living off-grid on his uncle Stanley's old farm out south. I asked Angel if she knew anything about Calisto.

"That the one with the tattoos?"

"Yeah. She said he was new around town. I think Calisto is really Thomas Richard "Harry" Harrison. He looked exactly like the guy in the mining picture, complete with big black beard. I'm thinking Kitty Love must be lying about not seeing him for years."

"Oh? Why?"

"This is Iron Creek, man. In case you haven't noticed. It's a small town. If Harrison is here, she would have at least heard about it or seen him at Cenex, or even just met him on the highway."

"She was young. People change."

Stanski eyeballed Davecki. "No they don't."

"Do." Davecki said. "Would you speed it up a little, Stan?"

Stanski laughed, satisfied that he'd finally gotten to Davecki. "I'm saving gas for the county, don't you know."

"Save it on your own time, buddy. I'm a busy man."

Stanski laughed. "Oh yeah, I forgot. You need to get home so you can play more Sudoku."

"Jerk."

Stanski returned to the question of Love being a liar. "That's another thing. She's gotta be in her forties. Maybe even fifties. If she hasn't seen Harrison since Alaska, how long ago was that?"

Davecki sighed. "I'll Google it. There had to be a news story about Carczak's disappearance. Or, at least there will be a date on record with Alaska Mining Claims," he said, pulling his phone.

"Something isn't adding up," Stanski said, piloting the car toward Davecki's F-150.

"Your math skills have long been suspect, pal."

"Pfft."

"No signal, as usual. I'll do the math for you. Let's say Love is forty-five. Nice in-between number for you. How old were Carczak and Harrison when they blazed a trail to Alaska?"

"In their twenties or so." Stanski steered the squad up to Davecki's F-150 so close it was impossible to open the passenger door.

"You so funny," Davecki said. He looked out at the snow-covered balsam trees, their shoulders sagging under the heavy weight of thick snow covering their limbs. "He was already married to Molly, right?"

Stanski drummed the steering wheel. "You know? He was, wasn't he?"

"Wonder why an up-and-coming vet would marry a loser like Carczak?"

Stanski drummed. "And then he takes off for Alaska with his buddy leaving a wife behind."

"Maybe a pregnant wife left behind," Davecki said. "Would you mind ceasing with the drumming thing? If it matters, you have sufficiently irritated me with it."

"Oh? I didn't realize."

"Right. I can understand if he and Harrison were facing heat here, they would want to get out of Dodge. Speaking of which, I'm eventually going to have to get out, you know."

"Oh? I didn't realize."

"You funny man."

The radio hissed, squawked, said, "Hayfield County 380. You there Stan?"

Stanski picked up the mic. "380. Hi, Michelle. What's up?"

"Caller on Tar Paper Alley said she's in the ditch. Her car ran out of gas while waiting for her husband to come pull her out. Baby on board and they're both getting cold."

"Ten-four. Tell her I can be there in fifteen."

"Ten-four."

Davecki popped the door open and bumped it against the side of the F-150.

"Hey! You're chipping the paint, man. Knock it off!"

"You mess with the bull, you get the horns."

"You're no fun." Stanski backed away from his joke, gave Davecki room to exit, said, "While I'm living a life of responsibility, you do the math. When I get a chance I'll check the FBI database for Harrison's release dates. How about you find out more about Calisto/Harrison? Pay him a friendly visit."

Davecki, one foot on the ground, one hand on the half-open

squad door, the other hand rubbing his chin, said, "Because I'm not cray-cray? Where would I find him?"

"Angel said he was hunkered down at his uncle's farm out south around Lake Chameek."

"Way out there? Down by the old Chauncy the Bear Hunter place?"

"Geez, Dave. At least shut the door, it's freezing out."

"Oh really? It's cold out, you say?" Davecki pushed the door out and back, pumping the frigid December air into Stanski's workspace.

"Knock it off, loser."

Davecki smirked, said, "Payback's a bitch, buddy." He got all the way out of the car and leaned back in, "And I'm to find this guy's place how?"

"Just use your superior detectivizing skills. You figured out where Kitty Love lives. The guy's uncle was Jacob Stanlayson or something like that."

"Oh, that's a solid lead."

"Quit complaining. You're the master detective. Try searching for Calisto or Harrison or Stanlayson or something."

"You're a big help. And once my superior detectivizing detects him, whatever am I to say upon my unannounced arrival at his off-grid camp that is likely heavily armed and ready for the zombie apocalypse? Um, excuse me Mr. Whoever You Are, but, would you mind telling me your real name, rank, and serial number?"

"Sounds reasonable to me," Stanski said. He reached to the heater controls, turned the fan and temp controller to blast furnace mode. "I gotta go, man. There's a freezing woman and child relying on my rapid response."

Davecki said, "Reasoning with an unreasonable person is like going to the hardware store for bread."

"You talking to me?" Stanski said. "You should talk. Your head has reasons that reason can't explain."

"Thanks," Davecki said.

Stanski fiddled with the heat controls again, looked at Davecki, "You're turning into a first-class wimp. You know that, don't you?"

"I'm not going to visit Calisto for you."

"For me? Aren't *you* curious?"

"Yes and no. I am curious to know about Kitty's lie, but I'm more motivated to let a sleeping dog lay or lie or whatever that rule is."

Stanski added, "Get in or out, just close the door, pal."

"I choose out," Davecki grinned. But he pumped the door a few more times.

"I'm going to have to kill you, Dave." Stanski floored the Dodge. The door slammed itself as the squad once again sprayed Davecki with snow and gravel, his hand in mid-air.

"Jerk," he mumbled, dusting snow and gravel off his Carhartt. Davecki turned a circle, taking in the snow-laden trees standing guard around the empty parking lot. Looks like a Hallmark Christmas card, he thought. Then he thought, you know? It is sorta cold.

In the pickup steaming down old Highway 97, he looked at the dashboard thermometer. Twenty below. Bit nippy, he thought. I wonder if Stan and Hawthorne are quits. Ahead, down the road, on the left side, Davecki saw the frenetic bounce of a single headlight coming at him. Damn ditch riders, they spend millions on snowmobile trails and goofballs won't use them. He realized the light didn't look like a snowmobile. Then he saw it was a dog team. What's Remington doing on the highway, he wondered.

Davecki's own keen grasp knew something was wrong when the unmistakable markings of Lead Dog Rampart led Remington's team whizzing past in the opposite direction. It wasn't Kaylee on the runners. It was a man. A tall man. Judging by the bushy beard peeking out of the parka-clad form hunched over the bow Davecki keenly grasped that it had to be either Angelo

Calisto or Harry Harrison.

Squinting in the outside rear view mirror, Davecki wondered, how can one musher get separated from her team so often? Slamming on the brakes, skidding, executing another super-fun reverse power turn, Davecki thought, well, well, well, the mountain has come to Muhammad.

CHAPTER 13

Heading south at speed on the Canadian slippy road in the still dusky gloaming of late afternoon-early evening, there was nary a dog team in sight as Davecki took his foot off the wood to keep from driving in a reckless and endangering manner. You never know when a State Stooper is lurking behind a side road's tall snowbank.

At the junction of Winneboujou and Highway 97, he had several choices. One was not asking a bystander, "Which way did they go?" There are no bystanders in December in Wisconsin's frozen north when the dashboard thermometer reads –22.

Or, he could guess.

Or, he could get out and look for tracks. Brr-cold, freeze-cold, he thought. Then he thought, maybe Stanski is right. I'm a wimp.

I could pray, I suppose, he reasoned.

"Jesus help me," Davecki mouthed.

Being no Jack Reacher, Jack Ryan, Jack Sparrow, Jack Bauer, or even Jack Frost, Davecki, unaided by fictional miracles coming to the rescue at just the right moment, skidded to a stop, slid out of the seat, ran in front of the pickup and, in the glow of the headlights, saw the slick narrow tracks of sled runners leading due south.

Back in the truck, as the horses under the hood did their thing, he wondered a thing or three. Maybe Molly was pregnant. Maybe Carczak didn't know he was going to be a father. Or maybe Kitty was just a kid at the time. Like Stan said, the timing is funky. More important, why did it matter? He thought of the advice Marshall Rosenblatt once gave him: *never answer a why question unless at least three lawyers are present*.

Speeding south, he recalled that Molly bought the watch in Nome. Or allegedly bought it in Nome. Maybe she reconciled with Carczak. Why am I always letting Stanski talk me into these wild goose chases? Where was Kaylee Remington? If she was adopted out in Alaska, that means Catherine Love was an Alaskan citizen, or at least she gave birth in Alaska. Where was Love and her Polaris? Pointing north somewhere? Lotta things pointing north in this case.

Was Calisto / Harrison fleeing? Maybe he was going for help? Out in the boonies of northern Wisconsin. Unlikely. Maybe the team was out of control and Calisto / Harrison got involved as he himself had the night before. Maybe the ex-con, ex-miner, ex-car thief, current mystery man hadn't turned dog-team-stealer. Maybe he was just holding on for dear life as he himself had done.

Speaking of deer. Just as the F-150 came around a corner at speed, a startled Bambi materialized in front of the truck as if by magic. One second, Davecki saw open frozen road, the next a slender brown arrow consisting of 150 pounds of grill-hood-fender-bashing Bambi. The fat fur ball sailed out from behind a nine-foot tall snowbank to land in the driving lane. Poor Bambi. It had three seconds to turn its muddled head and fulfill its clichéd role of, yes, *deer in the headlights.*

A deer's depth perception only works for the 60 degrees in

front of them where their field of vision overlaps with their peripheral vision. Plus as their pupils are wide and horizontal, they react more slowly than predator pupils.

The result?

WHAM! BAM! NO THANK YOU MA'AM!

Usually.

Davecki dodged the Ford around the deer, leaving it sniffing whiffs of eau de chrome from the outside rearview mirror going past its wet black nose with mere millimeters to spare.

Of course, there are consequences of avoiding "deer-vehicle encounters" as Bambi bashing is known in modern times. Specifically…the swerve. The swerve is the gateway drug to the fishtail. The fishtail leads to that dreaded opiate, oversteer. Oversteer leads to the slippy slope of plowing snow banks sans plow.

Davecki felt the weight of the watch on his wrist as he countersteered. Maybe the extra ounces saved his grill from becoming plastic hamburger after avoiding creating venison hamburger. Maybe his patrol training wasn't that rusty. Maybe his guardian angel's invisible but powerful fingers nudged the pickup just enough to keep it between the snowbanks.

Whatever the case may be, Davecki's trusty eight-cylindered F-150 did a 180 faster than Kristi Yamaguchi. In an instant Davecki was looking back the way he'd just come. The truck—brakes in full-lock-mode—skidded backward at speed. No amount of patrol car training can control a 60-MPH backslide. The 150 bounced its rear bumper off one of Rhoweder's snowbanks, entered a slo-mo spin, careened like an 8-ball into the other bank, spun around again and decided to face south once more.

"Cool," Davecki said as he put the sole to the wood. The F-150 shrugged the stress of the acrobatics off and shuddered south again.

"Atta girl," Davecki said, patting the "girl" on the steering wheel. I wonder if I can call a truck a girl? Have to ask Davina.

The fastest dog teams in the world cannot outrun even the

slowest pickups. Luckily Davecki wasn't driving a Brabus Unimog. In three minutes, the snow-covered backside of the musher appeared in the headlights. It looked like a white exclamation point against the now full-on darkness to the south.

In the glare of the lights Davecki saw Calisto or Harrison break Satchel Paige's number one rule: NEVER LOOK BACK. SOMEONE MIGHT BE GAININ' ON YOU.

It's hard to discern motive from two hundred feet away. The flurry of snow dust kicked up by forty clawed paws and two sled runners obscure the acuity of the moment. But, Davecki, using his highly-tuned grasp of the obvious, concluded that said musher, mushing down the wrong side of the highway, was uninterested in stopping for a chat. He tried the old flashing high-beams option, flicking them from high to low to high a half dozen times.

Musher X responded by waving his right arm in a come-around-idiot motion.

Davecki considered driving alongside the team and leaping from the truck like a cowboy hero of old leaping to the backs of a runaway stagecoach team. WWLD. What Would Longmire Do in this situation?

Lots of things wrong with the jumping out "pran" as Charlie Chan would say. As was usual with Davecki's charmed life, divine intervention intervened, as the department of redundancy department would say.

Or maybe Mr. Musher was unlucky.

Or maybe Rampart was smart. He decided to climb the snowbank. Maybe the salt on the road was too much for his toes. A good team trusts its lead dog. The whole string started clawing up Rhoweder's snowbank like there was fresh hot beaver carcass and beef heart on the topside.

Now, dogs are agile creatures. They have claws and paws that can dig and scratch for traction. They can't climb trees like fleeing bears hunted by hounds. Snow banks? Even Rhoweder-tall snow banks?

Definitely doable for a team of dogs.

Dog sleds? Not so much.

With the team topping the crusty snowbank, the sled nose bounced and banged halfway up. The long runners out back scraped against the roadway. Musher X ran like mad beside the tilted sled, hanging on to the bow like a Lake Chameek bloodsucker.

That guy is one tough SOB, Davecki thought, as F-150 slowed to watch the proceedings. The musher action was reminiscent of a sight gag in a Charlie Chaplin silent movie. "Whoa!" Davecki yelped, when all at once the sled boinged like a pogo stick to the top of the bank. Mr. Musher took one giant leap for musher-kind, sailed high, legs flailing air behind like a flag blowing in a twenty-knot wind. Magic ensued when Mr. Musher did a Simone Biles and stuck the landing square on the runners on top of the snowbank.

For brief seconds the sled and team kept pace with the truck. Mr. Musher looked right, directly at Dauntless Dave who now actually had to look up to return the astonishment. The big black beard covered with snow broke open, revealing an evil-looking sneer.

The connection lasted seconds as the fast Ford sped by the dog team. Davecki hit the brakes. The F-150, weighing approximately five thousand more pounds than the sled dog team, skidded long before stopping short on the slippy road.

Davecki jumped out of the truck and beat feet back to the epicenter of action. Just like Davecki to rush in where angels fear to tread. Some training never goes away for officers of the law, fire fighters, and other heroes like the front-line medical workers of the Covid pandemic.

As Davecki sprinted, Musher X hollered, "GEE, YOU HUSKIES!"

Rampart got the message and darted left.

Davecki scrambled up the snowbank. Made a diving grab for

the sled's rear stanchion. The team careened down a ditch rider's snowmobile track.

Why am I doing this? Davecki asked the not-present-three-lawyers as he caught hold.

Banging along on his backside, snow being injected down the back of his Carhartt while clinging to the dog sled with gloveless hands in 25-below temperatures, while simultaneously being kicked by a big sized-thirteen boot will discourage the most ardent pursuer of truth, justice, and the diminishing-in-stature American Way.

Being more than ardent by several factors and fractals, Davecki managed to hang on for three, maybe four minutes. Or, maybe it was fifteen seconds. Time passes slowly when you're having fun. Whatever the case, Davecki ended up face down in the snow listening to the swish of departing sled runners.

In certain situations, snow can be very comforting. Like when a person is freezing to death and the well-documented sense of being hot causes hypothermia victims to shed their clothing to be found naked and stiff as a Popsicle, and, by the by, quite dead.

Davecki took solace in the snow, laying there for a few seconds, or perhaps three or four minutes, time passes slowly when you're retired, out of shape, and have just exerted yourself more than at any time in recent, or even distant, memory. He rolled to his back and studied the distant stars. He shook his bare hands free of snow and tucked them under his armpits. The cold air stung his nose and singed his lips as he gasped for breath and took in the heavenly view. He took stock of his body. Everything seemed okay. No major pains.

Maybe I'm not too old for this after all, he thought. Getting a little adrenaline into my bloodstream feels pretty good. "Hah!" he said to the black sky and stars above. "Hah! Hah! Hah!" he yelped some more. If I were a wolf I'd howl.

What the hey?! Nobody around to care.

I'm a wolf.

He lifted his chin and howled, "WOOoooOOOooo! WOOoooOOOooo! WOOoooOOOooo!"

That felt great. Now I know why wolves and dogs howl. It feels so good. "WOOoooOOOooo! WOOoooOOOooo! WOOoooOOOooo!"

"WOOoooOOOooo," he howled at the Big Dipper, Polaris and Orion. One thing about howling, it requires a lot of air. Breathing heavily, he sat up, shook his head at his foolishness.

His shame sharpened when Stanski's voice came from the darkness asking, "I know you're out there somewhere, Davecki. I heard your pathetic wolf imitation."

Davecki looked in the direction of Stanski's voice. Saw the approaching black blob that loomed tallish and thick against the whiteness of the snow and the thinness of the surrounding tree stems. The black blob wielded a light-saber-like flashlight beam.

"Here, boss," Davecki said.

"For crying out loud, Dave. You trying to commit suicide by stupidity or something?"

"No, Stan, I'm not. I'm just having a sweet little winter picnic to pass the long night." Davecki struggled to his feet, finding footing on the packed track of the snowmobiler's trail.

Stanski trudged up, said, "You can get yourself real frost-bitten out here, Dave. You know that, don't you?"

Dusting snow off his knees, Davecki said, "You worry too much, buddy. If I'd got in real trouble I'd just Carole King out your name on 911 and you'd come running to save me again."

"Oh, you mean with this cell phone?" Stanski said, handing Davecki his phone. "The one on the ground next to your idling pickup parked across a full lane of traffic?"

"Oh. Huh. Thanks, Patrick," Davecki said. "Yes, officer. You are right, officer. It was foolish of me to leave my vehicle idling in the middle of the road blocking all the super-high volumes of traffic rushing past at this time of year at this time of night in super-densely-populated Hayfield County. How foolish of me to try to be of help foiling the commission of a crime."

The loving couple turned as one to slip-slide through snow back toward their vehicles.

"Crime? There's been a crime committed without my knowledge?"

"Yes, officer, I witnessed it myself. Grand theft doggo."

"Huh," Stanski said. "Guess that explains the two irate women on the Polaris back on the road."

"How'd you get here so fast? Thought you were heading for a mother and child reunion?"

"It was only a motion away. Dispatcher Michelle called. Said the husband showed. Then another mother and child, this time on a snowmobile, flagged me down."

CHAPTER 14

Back at the convocation of the patient, idling F-150, the steady, reliable Dodge Squad, and the aged but still firm Polaris snow sled, super-intense Kitty Love, confused-looking Kaylee Remington, and Stanski held a social distance meeting. Nobody wore masks.

"How could you let him get away with our dog team?" Kitty Love asked. Her round face took on an angular aspect, eyebrows arched under Redpaw stocking hat. Eyes narrowed. Jaw set. Lips trending toward white around the edges.

Stanski angled himself toward the area between the two women.

"He just jumped out of the woods like a mad man and tackled Rampart," Kaylee Remington said. "He pushed me down and hiked the team down the trail. If Kitty hadn't come along, I'd still be walking."

They weren't that obedient for me, Davecki thought.

"How could you let him get away?" Remington asked. She squared her shoulders toward Stanski, shot a look of doom at Davecki.

Davecki saw Stanski stifle a laugh. Instead the Deputy turned face on to Davecki, said, "Yes, Alphonse, how could you let him get away?"

No good deed goes unpunished, Davecki, thought. "It was easy," he said, "All I had to do was let him kick me until I let go."

"You guys think this is some sort of joke?" Love asked. Her jaw muscles flexed like Glint Westwood in the movie *Fistful of Pocket Change.*

Stanski flicked a "jerk" look at his old partner, then looked at the women and said, "I apologize. Sometimes I get a little too funny. I'm sorry. We're here to help, ladies. Backup is coming. Meanwhile Mr. Davecki here did his best to help out and I'm sure he made quite an impression on Mr. Calisto. Once our backup arrives with the proper snow-going equipment we will pursue the perpetrator with all good diligence and get to the bottom of this."

"Calisto?" Love repeated. "Who in the world is Calisto?"

"According to Mr. Davecki's description," Stanski continued in his everything-is-under-control-calming-voice-of-reassurance from his conflict resolution classes, "The man who stole the dog team in question is the man I met at Cenex last week named Angelo Calisto. Big black beard. About five ten. Couple hundred pounds?" He looked at Davecki.

"That about covers it," Davecki said. Except for the size sixteen boots, he thought. He rubbed his arm. At least that's what they felt like as they tried to break my arm, he thought again. Is this the first-ever instance of a dog-jacking, Davecki wondered.

Love looked the men over, cast a sidewise glance at Remington. Her face, in the glow of headlights from the squad and patiently idling F-150, revealed that a quick decision had been made, "I know nothing of any Angelo Calisto. It had to be that rotten Harry Harrison."

Davecki stared straight at Love, refusing to look at Stanski. After being partners for so long, Davecki knew Stanski wore his, *I am SO smart,* look. Don't give him the satisfaction, Davecki urged himself. His head is fat enough.

"You mean Harry Harrison, your father's old partner?" Stanski asked.

Love huffed. Glared at Stanski. "Are you dense or something? That's exactly who I mean."

"I thought you hadn't seen him for years," Stanski said.

"I haven't. Still haven't. According to Kaylee and Mr. Wiseacre there," she jerked her head toward Davecki, "It has to be Harrison."

"Why would he want to steal a dog team?" Stanski rubbed the back of his neck.

Kaylee Remington looked directly at Love, raised eyebrows placing the same question on her face.

"Because he's a mean S.O.B. who hates all things Carczak and would do anything to ruin our Iditarod chances. Plus, he knows how much our dogs are worth. If he's hurting for money, which he always is, he could sell them for big bucks."

"Oh no!" Remington said.

"Don't worry, m..." Stanski saved himself from saying ma'am and pivoted in an instant to "...my backup will track the team down."

Davecki said, "The man I tried to stop told Deputy Stanski his name was Angelo Calisto."

"That's bull roar," Love said. "It's Harry. Had to be."

A siren sound seeped into the conversation, coming from far away down Highway 97 to the north.

"Time's wasting," Love said. "We're going after him. They're our dogs." She turned toward the Polaris in the background.

"Ma'am, this is a police matter now," Stanski said, not realizing he used the m-word.

"Oh, great. I'm brimming with confidence," Love griped. "You must be dense. How many times I got to tell you to quit calling me ma'am?"

Stanski looked toward Davecki.

"So," Davecki said, "I'm confused. The guy I chased told Stan his name was Calisto. You're saying he's really your father's old partner Harry Harrison. And you think his motive for taking the team is to ruin your Iditarod run. Correct?"

"That's what I'm saying," Love said. "And to cash in on our breeding and training. Lots of rich musher wanna-bes rent teams to run the race. They fly in a couple of weeks before and become insta-mushers."

Stanski stepped away, moving toward his squad.

"Revenge. Spite. Hate," Love answered. Her look followed Stanski as he moved off. The side of her neck peeked out from her parka.

Only three? Davecki thought. She forgot greed. "What happened up in Alaska that made him so angry? So desperate?"

Remington, again turned her face toward Love, eyebrows raised.

Love hesitated, huffed a little. Davecki knew the signs of quick mental editing going on under that stocking cap. He'd seen it hundreds of times in interview rooms as perps made quick context checks in their stories.

"The loser quit Dad's mine before the big pay. When Dad struck it rich, Harry came crawling back wanting his share. Dad gave him a poke of gold and told him to never come around again."

Harrison's name is still on the claim, Davecki remembered. "That's it? How much was the poke worth?"

"At the time probably around ten grand," Love said.

Seems like a lot of hate over ten grand, Davecki thought.

Love turned and glanced at the arriving Hayfield County truck-squad pulling a shiny new aluminum rail-trailer loaded with a huge Bombardier four-wheeler equipped with super expensive tracks instead of tires. "Oh, great. The big boys with their expensive toys have arrived," she said.

Davecki resisted his penchant for distraction and stayed with the theme, "So, Harrison ditched your dad. Your dad struck it rich and now Harrison posing as Calisto steals your team to punish you for being his ex-partner's daughter and to possibly sell or rent the team to an Iditarod poser? Seems like, I don't know... complicated. And petty? And, probably impossible considering how will he explain suddenly having an Iditarod ready team available?"

Love reached up, pulled her stocking cap off, stuffed it in a parka pocket. "You some sort of mushing expert all of a sudden?" She unzipped her parka a little.

She's hot, Davecki thought. Hell hath no fury, he pondered.

"Plus, that's Harry's style. Mean-spirited and small minded."

She called him Harry, Davecki thought. That seems awfully familiar. Studying her neck, he thought, no chicken neck. She's younger than I thought. Wonder how old she is? Not fifty I bet. No crow's feet. Maybe not even forty.

"What are you staring at, Bozo?" Love asked. She zipped up the parka.

Davecki pivoted to the Remington view. Wonder how old she is? Thirty? If daughter is like mother, she may be younger than first impressions. Could be late twenties. Wonder how old Love was when she gave birth?

Stanski returned from consulting with the consulting deputy who was consulting with the tie-down straps holding the boy-toy to the trailer.

The pulsing red lights against the snow and dark sky and naked trees reminded Davecki of *Judge Dredd*. One of those flying squads would come in handy right now, he thought. Too cold though. The puffs of steam coming out of each speaker's mouth whenever they spoke reminded Davecki of *Game of Thrones.* How fake the winter scenes were. Though a dragon would make a handy squad right now, wouldn't it? Built in hand and butt warmer chasing down a dog-jacker in the middle of winter.

"We'll track your team down, ladies. I have your cell number. I'll call you when we catch him," Stanski said.

Davecki pulled out his cell. He twisted it, lifted it above his head. "No reception."

"This whole area is a dead zone," Remington said. "I've been mushing every trail between here and Lake Superior for weeks. There are only a few high spots with a signal."

"I've got a sat phone for backup," Stanski said, hoisting the canvas tote in his left hand.

"Where do you people get all your money?" Love asked.

"Umm, taxes?" Davecki suggested.

"Don't get cute with me," Love said.

She's upset. Don't take it personally, Davecki thought. It says more about her than me. Then he said, "My feet are cold. I'm going to warm up."

Sitting behind the wheel watching the law enforcement wheels go 'round, Davecki wondered how Hawthorne was doing. Heavy sigh. Who needs a hottie when you've got a hot truck? He sighed again, laid his weary head back against the headrest, shrugged his shoulders, winced in pain as his right rotator cuff informed him it was extremely unhappy with recent unreasonable performance requests. "Lord, help me," Davecki mumbled a prayer. Just about to doze off, a knock on the window, startled him.

"Get some rest, Dave," Stanski said before the power window was all the way down. "I'll call you when we get him."

"You're a good man, Stan," Davecki grinned.

"Quit messing around, Dave."

"Seriously. You're doing a good job in a difficult situation. I liked how you conducted yourself just now," Davecki said.

"It's all about the training, man."

"Pfft. It's all about the trainee." Davecki looked at the black woods. "Take it easy out there. Harrison seems like he could be dangerous."

"I'm thinking Love is over-reporting his threat."

"Tell that to my arm and shoulder."

Stanski laughed a little. “Seems sort of normal to not want someone dragging alongside your dogsled.”

“Silly me,” Davecki laughed a little. “Either way, take care out there.” He nodded toward the big black beyond out in the woods where strange things can happen.

“Will do, mildew,” Stanski said, turning away to his responsibilities.

Davecki ran the window up, put the truck in gear, eased through the congestion of officialdom studying the convocation on the side of the road where Kitty Love gesticulated as Stanski stood by. The backup deputy sat patiently on the ready-and-waiting-track-equipped quad. Remington watched him roll past. She nodded in his direction. Davecki lifted his finger from the steering wheel in the Northland Salute, nodded back at Remington, and followed his headlights into the darkness.

Driving along in his automobile, feelings of relief swept him. “Thank you, Jesus.” He was grateful he could go home and sauna instead of having to chase around the boonies looking for a dog team in a haystack, or something like that.

CHAPTER 15

Standing on battered blue flip-flops, naked as a newborn, twenty below, looking up at the black sky above, the crystal-clear twinkling stars again informed Davecki that life was worth living. Maybe I shouldn't be so hard on you, body. You're a good body. The steam and heat from said cooling flesh flowed past his grizzled jaw and fatigue-lined face in waves he could feel, see and smell. Upwards toward the immense black sky, miniscule human heat passed, also informing him of his insignificance. Davecki wondered at the miracle of sauna. Lifting his arm, it didn't hurt at all. It was right and good to see the steam radiating from skin to sky. Shrugging his shoulders, the clavicle brothers clicked and clacked against the muscle tension the sauna hadn't reached. It was quite a jolt, grabbing on to that moving sled, being dragged and kicked. Thank you, body, he thought, for being so tough and strong and resilient and enduring and with only minor complaints of old age compared to the suffering so many go through.

Thank you, sauna, he thought looking at the hot little shed sitting strong and resilient itself, refusing to bow to winter, steadfastly saying to old man winter, "Ain't no thang."

Don't start with the thang thing, Davecki advised the part of himself that found punning irresistible, and, once started, addictive.

Dyslexic mind rambling, he thought…great to have sauna in winter in Wisconsin. The dead of winter, some say. Why not, the "alive" of winter? That was a hard one. What's the opposite of dead? Sensing the subtle transition between being invincibly hot against the twenty-below, and the cold getting the best of flesh, he left the stars to their own devices, reentered sauna and reveled in the 122 degrees.

Seating himself on the highest bench, Davecki gripped and dipped a scoop of water from the wooden bucket. He flipped the ladle just so and the water hit the hot rocks, hissing and spitting from liquid to gas. As the searing wave front swept his skin, he took mini breaths against the blistering storm, his nostrils cringing at the sting.

I wonder what Harrison's really up to, Davecki wondered. There's got to be more than destroying an Iditarod run. That's just spite or hate. Or even making a bundle renting out a stolen team. Maybe I should dive into the snow and roll around like the old days. Not. He dismissed the urge to be young again, replacing it with, Love sure seems complicated. Her bedside manner, so to speak, leaves a lot to be desired. Probably loves animals way more than humans. Back to Harrison. Why give an alias to Stanski? Knee jerk reaction of a career criminal seeing squad and uniform? Could he really make a bundle renting a stolen dog team? How could he pull that off? Wouldn't everyone up there in Iditarod land know the team was hot? And how much could he make? A few thousand? Lots of risk and effort for that kind of a payday.

If Harrison is as rough on the inside as he looks on the outside, he'll be a worthy adversary for Stanski. Glad I don't have to worry about that now, Davecki comforted himself, reaching for the silver dipper again. Love's acidity seems over the top, he thought as he tossed more water to death on the rocks.

The thermometer in the corner only went to 130 degrees. The red needle was well past that mark. "I give," Davecki mumbled. He climbed down from the top bench, dumped the water from the bucket on the hot rocks and fled the onslaught of steam chasing him out the sauna door. Walking to the trailer, immune to the cold, he thought, this is great. Cold be damned. Thank you, blue plastic slippers for keeping my soles from freezing. Thank you, hot skin for keeping my old heart from freezing. From seizing up in this old body. Huh, he thought, my body isn't really me. But then again it is. Huh.

Exactly equidistant between trailer and sauna, headlights turning into the driveway brought a more earthly concern to Davecki's cosmic pondering. Run back to the sauna? Run to the trailer? Who would be coming down the driveway? The FedEx lady? UPS? The FBI? Like a deer in headlights, Davecki stood stunned. Wish I had a towel at least, he thought, and then he heard the rumble and breathed a sigh of relief.

Mr. Dodge Squad rolled to a stop. The window powered down. "You know I can't unsee this," Stanski complained.

"That's your just punishment for encroaching unannounced on a person's privacy unannounced," Davecki said.

"Enough with the redundancy joke. I called. You didn't answer."

"I'm not addicted to the phone like you. It's in the trailer."

"You ever hear of this modern invention called a towel?" Stanski asked.

"What's that?" Davecki answered, looking around. Steam rose from his flesh in mini waves of heat.

"It's like a robe, only smaller," Stanski said, popping his door.

"Shut that thing down," Davecki said, turning toward the trailer. "You're wasting gas and adding carbon to my lovely night sky."

"Can't," Stanski said, following, "too many electronics that need power."

"So you're the one to blame for climate change."

"Pfft," Stanski said. "You didn't get the memo that global warming is a hoax?"

"You're right of course. Global warming *is* a hoax. But climate change is real, nimrod," Davecki said, opening the porch door.

"So now you're a climatologist?" Stanski asked, stomping his boots on the entry room floor.

"Compared to you, I'm an expert on everything. And, for the record, whatever it is you want, Stan, the answer is no."

CHAPTER 16

Inside the trailer, Davecki's heart went clang, clang, clang as Stanski reported, "We couldn't find him. Weird. But it was like he evaporated. Kitty Love said that her dad had a cabin up near Lake Superior that nobody was supposed to know about but that everyone knew about."

Pulling his boots on, Davecki wondered if it was the big one making his heart do jumping jacks. Or was it the fright from being nabbed naked in the night?

"Why are you dragging me into this? I'm retired, don't you know."

Stanski grinned, "That's the point. The cabin is on the Bois Brûlé Reservation. No jurisdiction."

"The FBI has jurisdiction. Why aren't you bothering Brekken?"

"She would have to alert the Tribal Police. It would blow her cover. You on the other hand, will be just a private citizen out for an innocent health hike in the wondrous Wisconsin woods. No problem. No suspicions. Few questions asked."

Davecki stood, pulled his Carhartt off the back of the kitchen chair, and, belying his disdain for Stanski's plan, headed for the door, saying, "Like some old fart wandering around the snowmobile trails on Reservation land in the middle of the night in the middle of winter won't raise an eyebrow."

"Precisely, mon frère. Precisely."

"You're an idiot. Your plan stinks. But I'm sick of watching PBS reruns. So, let's get this fool's errand under way."

"I love you too, Davy. Oh, by the way. We have to take your truck. The squad would get unwanted attention."

"Jerk."

Underway Davecki asked, "Why not just call the Tribal Police?"

"Because it's no big deal at this point. If it weren't for that watch, it would just be a dispute between neighbors, or at least, grand theft doggo. Calling the TP would complicate things unnecessarily."

"You're right about that. The fewer people know about the watch the better. At least until we find out if it's real or fake," Davecki said. They rode along in silence until he added, "You're asking a lot of a private citizen."

"Suck it up, Buttercup."

Physically, reservation land looks like every other wild acreage in Hayfield County. But, by dint of treaty, one minute you're in America, the next you're in another sovereign nation, a different culture, and a foreign jurisdiction.

Stanski's face glowed pale white from the glow of his phone. He looked at Davecki, then ahead. "No signal, but back a few miles Google Maps said the Bumbleaxe Snowmobile Trail is up ahead. When you see the next trail crossing, pull over."

"Whatever you say, Boss." Davecki slowed the truck, glanced at Stanski, asked, "Then what?"

"Just hoof it down the trail. Look for dog team tracks. See if there's any place where a dog team veers off into the woods."

A diamond-shaped yellow warning sign with a snowmobile on it appeared in the headlights. Davecki slowed the truck more. "You ever look at that sign?"

"Gee Dave, in twenty years of patrol I've never ever seen a snowmobile crossing sign," Stanski answered.

"Jerk. Doesn't it seem weird to you?"

"No why?"

"Well, look at it. The guy on the snowmobile is like a giant compared to the machine."

Stanski bent forward, studying the sign as it went past. "Huh. Never noticed that before. That's why you're such a good detective."

"Retired."

"Oh yeah, that."

"Stan, why not just call the T.P.? Have them do your dirty work for you?"

"I will. But this is too sketchy yet. If you find Harrison, I'll call 'em right away."

"It's your show."

"If you bump into the T.P. just tell them you fell off the back of your buddy's machine and are walking in the direction he went until he comes back for you."

"Implausible."

Stanski asked, "Why's that?"

"Wouldn't a snowmobile drive know if the passenger suddenly wasn't there?"

"Not the bar hoppers. At least not right away. That's what makes it plausible."

"Just barely," Davecki said.

"You're a good boy, Davy."

"Woof. Woof."

"You so funny. I'll come back to pick you up in half an hour. If you find dog team tracks heading north off the trail we'll get the T.P. and go collar him."

"We're going to a lot of effort based on Kitty Love's recollection. She strikes me as duplicitous."

"Duplicitous? You reading Tom Wolfe again?"

"No. Shakespeare and Ed Newman."

"Why you think Love is strange?" Stanski asked as Davecki stopped the truck next to the snowmobile trail.

"The lady doth protest too much, methinks."

"She's a busy lady with a lot on her mind and her puppies are gone missing."

"There's that," Davecki said as he popped his door. Before putting boots on ground, he said, "This is cray-cray. You know that, right?"

"What's your problem, man? You used to love all this backcountry, wilderness, wild-ass Daniel Boone stuff. Who was that new hero you had? Some mountain man, wasn't it?"

"Dick Summers," Davecki said, putting boots on ground.

Stanski popped his door, walked around the front of the truck. Snow started falling from the black sky above. Big fat fluffy flakes wafted downward like soft feathers falling from the angel pillow fight above. He looked up, blinked, said, "Lake effect snow as usual." He jumped into the Ford, slammed the door, powered down the window, grinned and said, "See you in half an hour."

As the red glare of the truck's taillights receded, Davecki thought, I wonder what the Eskimo word for big fat fluffy snow is? Hoofing down the trail, he yanked his black Newlich Implement stocking cap from the Carhartt pocket and pulled it down over his ear tops. From the other pocket, the headlamp. Adjusting the headlamp a little, he switched it on and zipped the jacket up tighter to his neck. Walking from the road to the snowmobile trail he thought, one small step for not-really-law-enforcement, a giant leap for a fool's errand.

Every fool's errand has silver linings. Like the hypnotic fall of big snowflakes passing through a headlamp beam. The total silence of walking at night when sound is dampened by snow everywhere. Like human eyes adjusting to the available light and switching off the headlamp to walk along in utterly enveloping silence and a mellow darkness gently illuminated by white snow in all directions. Like the beauty of naked trees rising from the thick carpet of snow undulating off to infinity and beyond; the tiny crinkling feeling of freezing eyelashes busting free of one another upon blinking; the soft touch of fat snowflakes landing on hot cheeks; the warmth building in the chest as the walk generates heat; the unzipping of the jacket as the body dares the cold to defy the internal combustion of well-fed organs, hot blood pumping strong, and the strength of flesh against the elements.

Looking at the naked trees, listening to the crunch-crunch of boots on snow, Davecki thought, this is nice…stupid…but nice.

"Skritch, skritch, skritch," the boots said. Why would Kitty Love even tell Stanski about the alleged hunting shack on reservation land when the deputies returned dog team-less? Ding, ding, ding went the alarm bells in his head. How in the world could a dog team evade modern technology and the pursuit of multi-million-dollar equipped deputies?

Looking up through the witch-finger trees, he thought, I bet there is intelligent life just on the other side of that impossible distance. I bet they're watching how we do as a human race. Walking on into the wild he thought of Jon Krakauer and Chris McCandless. What a fool McCandless was. No more than me, he thought, rescuing Stanski like this. We should just get the T.P. and go about this the right way. On the other hand, it is lovely out. It's lovely being warm inside good clothing. What do the Norwegians say? There's no such thing as bad weather. Only bad clothing. It's nice being protected from the cold. It's nice being able to see ghostly shadows that exist only when the glow of snow-light hints at their presence. I wonder if Winneboujou the trickster is afoot on the reservation tonight. This is nice. Nice, nice, nice.

The eyes have it, Davecki told himself as he stared hard into the blue-gray darkness created in the interface of the white snow and the dark sky above. There it is again, he said to himself. A flicker of yellow between the interlacing frozen tree stems weaving the earth and sky together like a willow basket holding the cosmos together.

That's the Winneboujou ancient legend, right? The universe is a big willow basket filled with galaxies being carried by Nanabozho? Lord, forgive me for not knowing my native folklore better. Gotta take a class or something.

Again, a flicker of yellow in the dark distance through the trees. A cabin light? Looks more like a flame.

It's a known fact, well established by years and years of research, experience, and good fiction…light, and Winneboujou, plays tricks with eyes at night. Davecki blinked, rubbed his eyes with the back of both mittened hands, blew the fog of his breath down and away from his line of vision and moved his head forth and back. But the flicker of yellow was not to be seen.

"Humpf," he said. He resumed shuffling along the snowmobile trail. Maybe I should turn on my headlamp. No, that will give me away. I wonder if Harrison is armed and dangerous. Me without my Kimber. I could probably take him in a fight. Maybe. I'm thinking too much. Anticipation is always worse than reality.

Wait! There's the light again. As he walked, the yellow flashed into and out of sight like a grouse fleeing an owl, twisting and turning through the trees.

The closer to the yellow flicker, the larger it appeared. And now it wasn't moving away, but it was moving in the sense of jumping, leaping, dancing.

"ON BY!" a man's bellow came out of the darkness down the trail straight ahead.

In the next instant, Davecki instinctively jumped aside as Rampart, Roosevelt, Reiny, Rembrandt, Rocket, Radar, Rivka, and the rest of the R's undulated past, pulling against their tug lines. In the next next instant, Remington's sled appeared like a fright-house skeleton jumping out of a dark corner.

At the last second Davecki saw the fist coming. He did an excellent imitation of Keanu Reeves in *The Matrix,* leaning backwards like a limbo dancer avoiding having his cold nose socked by the onrushing musher's stiff-arm.

Unlike the movie, Davecki didn't have invisible strings helping him defy gravity. Landing flat on his back, all the air in his lungs huffed out like a balloon popping. Like the big muskie of late, Davecki jawed unsuccessfully for oxygen. As the synapses and autonomic responses responsible for normal breathing did the chicken dance trying to get in synch, Davecki noted the witch-finger tree limbs above grasping unsuccessfully at the stars.

Beautiful.

Also of note to Davecki was his body flip-flopping between life and death from oxygen deprivation. The third note in the chord was the whispering sound of swishing sled runners on the frozen snow as the miscreant made yet another slippy getaway.

Death be not proud, Davecki prayed as he gasped. He twisted to his right and curled into a fetal position wondering if Donne or Gunther ever had problems like this. I should have become a writer instead of a cop, he managed to think in the seconds before the flashing of bright white lights appeared like the locomotive at the end of the tunnel.

Then the roar of the snowmobile's sound traveling slightly slower than Mach 1 arrived. Davecki's poor brain and body. He had no chance. Being run over by a snowmobile is no fun. But there are a few advantages to be had even in the most extreme situations. Heavy layers of clothing including thick Carhartts and boots. Snow, even the snow of a groomed trail, is softer than asphalt or concrete. And then there's the instinctive reaction of the sled driver upon seeing a curled human form on the side of the trail in the middle of the Rez in the middle of winter in the middle of the wilderness of wild Wisconsin.

Naturally any driver wants to avoid smashing their fifteen thousand-dollar jewel of modern winter recreation technology into a blob of huddling human flesh, thus injuring the poor machine.

And then there's the instinctive reaction of a soon-to-be hit-and-run victim scratching away from imminent doom.

The blessing in all this?

Instead of splattering Davecki parts all over the snow the speeding sled just ran over Davecki's left foot.

Any drunken snowmobile driver worth their salt, having experienced running over a human foot in the middle of the woods would do the right thing of course. That is: leave the scene post haste. In life as we know it, nothing but complications await the conscientious, so why mess up a bar-hopping drunken beer-and-booze bender with something resembling responsibility?

Under the influence of a greater priority, Davecki's body figured out how to breath fast, deep, and furious as the pain in his foot/ankle sent urgent messages to the far distant brain, clearing away the fog and inducing instant focus.

"Owie! Owie! Owie!" Davecki yelled to nobody. If a dumbass gets run over in the woods and nobody hears his pitiful squeals, is there actually sound and fury?

Yes.

Davecki pushed on his elbows like a grasshopper until his back came into contact with the plowed-up snowbank from Willie Scott's trail grooming. Resting and trying to will the pain in his miserable limb to subside, he growled through gritted teeth, "Now what?" With fat snowflakes landing and melting on his overheated face he concluded that, yes, indeed, a Sequoia had fallen in the woods.

Many instants and moments and segments of time passed with Davecki's consciousness coming and going with the pain. His breathing regulated itself. The pain-blurred vision regained some acuity. The falling snow increased in density, accumulating on the lap of his legs. He discovered that flopping his foot left and right was only semi-torturous. With each slow flop of his left foot, he looked in the same direction down the trail. Staring into the darkness to the south the way the dog team had gone…only the blackness of the void that-a-way. To the north he looked. No sign of mechanized mayhem returning to finish the job a la *Easy Rider*.

Flinching around the stabs of pain that shot up his leg as he moved, he managed to get to the all-fours position old dogs are familiar with. Breathing through his mouth against the pain of the cold air in his nostrils, he did sad donkey / angry cat. "That's better," he consoled himself, having found in the yoga maneuver the will to live. Sad ass is more like it, he thought.

A few more sad Davecki donkey / angry cats had him fixed up enough to struggle to his feet. Or, rather, foot. Standing with arms wind-milling attempting to stave off falling over, Davecki put a little pressure on his left foot and found that he could hobble / hop.

I wonder how far in I walked? Couple of miles maybe. Stanski will be wondering what happened to me. Or he'll see Harrison and initiate pursuit. I wish another snowmobiler would come along and give me a ride. Or maybe run me over for real and finish the job.

He looked up, and, managing to remain upright, he chanted, "Lord, I need a little help here, Buddy. How about a rescuing angel?" He stuck out his tongue. Lapped at more falling snowflakes. "I'd settle for another snowmobile, Lord," he added.

Hearing his own voice crying in the wilderness made him laugh out loud. He recalled his mother saying, "Don't get yourself in a pickle and don't bring the cops down on us," when going out to play with Jackie and Mikey and Rudy. The memory prompted a sob and self-pity. No way, he thought, I got myself into this pickle, I'll get myself out. Shaking his head to shake off the lure of defeatism he noticed again the yellow flicker that had ignited all this drama. The flicker was now a flame. Keen grasper of the obvious, Davecki concluded that there was a fire the size of a Mack truck going like, well, like blazes, about three hundred yards off the trail.

The snow off the trail was crotch deep. There has to be an Eskimo word for crotch-deep-snow, he thought. Swim/wading through actually lessened the pain in his left foot. I think I can, I think I can, he *Little Engine That Could*(ed) himself toward the fire. Then he struck the dog team track. Progress came easier. Thank you team for packing a track.

Sweating from the exertion and pain he unzipped his Carhartt to cool off. Accumulated snow fell from his shoulders. Remington was right, he thought, by the yard, it's hard. Inch by inch it's a cinch. Closing in on the blaze he realized it was once a cabin or a shack about the size of the aforementioned Mack truck. Maybe twelve by twenty feet at most. Now it was a loose assembly of blazing walls about to collapse. The heat feels good on my face, Davecki thought. After a few seconds he spun a 180 to warm his backside. Must be what the dark side of the moon feels like all the time, he thought.

Then he thought, man I'm tired. He did what Dick Summers would not have done. He sat down in the snow and fell asleep in an instant.

CHAPTER 17

Dawn comes slowly in the north of Wisconsin in December and it comes weakly with light angling in at 23.5 degrees. Davecki's wake cycle mimicked the dawn. Awareness trudged along like walking in waist-deep water, which is what he was dreaming of, walking in waist deep turquoise sea water on a Caribbean beach. In the dream he stepped on a sea urchin. That dream pain woke him to his real pain. Wish I had some champagne, he thought, brushing twelve inches of fluffy snow off his chest.

Rising up like a whale breaching, he saw even more snow falling. He rolled left, plowing snow as he went. Ripping and tearing sounds from below as his Carhartts separated from the ice he'd formed while sleeping.

"My foot doesn't hurt," he lied out loud, to make the false claim ring true. He grabbed the nearest maple sapling and struggled to his feet, or actually his foot and a half.

Good to hear a voice, he thought, even if it's my own. Blinking against the dawn, the snowflakes frozen to his eyelashes crinkled and crashed and melted on his cheek. "Brr-cold, freeze-cold," he said as he slapped his sides with his hands to get some circulation going. Tottering and slapping himself, I wonder what the Eskimo equivalent of brr-cold-freeze-cold is. To avoid toppling over, he put undue pressure on his left foot.

"Owie! Owie! Owie!" he yelped. He looked around in fear. Oh yeah, I'm alone in the middle of the woods in the middle of the Rez in the middle of a northern Wisconsin blizzard and in a real pickle. Nobody here to hear.

He grabbed the handy maple sapling and took more pressure off his left foot. He moved the damaged foot slowly through the fresh snow, stirring the fluffy stuff like powdered sugar in a bowl. He swatted at the snow that had melted to the front of his Carhartt. The ice that had formed around his collar overnight from his shallow breathing cracked and fell through his V-neck and shocked the skin around his Adam's apple.

"Sheesh," he said leaning forward. Good thing Rip Van Winkle didn't wake up in December, he thought. I wonder if I'm going to get out of here alive. The ankle injury isn't going to kill me, but this snow and the cold might. He looked at the impression his body had made in the snow and realized he'd broken a cardinal, or at least a bishop, rule and was blessed to have awakened.

Looking further afield, the falling snow parted now and then, revealing a thick horse's tail of dirty smoke rising from the black circle where the cabin fire smoldered. All that remained were black boards, ashes, the hulk of a stove, and the stark outline of what were once steel-legged kitchen-type chairs. The debris field fought a losing battle against the falling snow. Beyond the former cabin he saw an old-fashioned outhouse. Atop the slanted outhouse roof, four feet of snow and growing. The surrounding trees looked like raw recruits standing at stiff attention awaiting inspection. There was no sky at all. Only an all-enveloping gray with heavy snow falling in sheets.

He shifted his weight, can't stand long with this bad leg, he thought. Then he thought, nobody's going to find my tracks, with this much snow there are no tracks. Unzipping his Carhartt, he discovered what he already knew, no cell signal plus low battery warning. Holding his phone above his head was futile and difficult considering he was balancing on one leg and holding hands with a supple sapling. Stanski's got a problem too, he considered. No doubt a snow emergency has been called. He'll be doing double duty rescuing stranded travelers. Plus, I'm officially unofficial and on Rez land without permission. He can hardly call out the National Guard to start a search. He looked around. It was all blizzard all the time. "Got myself in a real pickle here, Ma," he said, to no one that disagreed.

Man, I'm hungry.

No you're not, he tried mind over matter.

The gut doesn't lie. The gnawing continued.

Nope. I'm hungry.

So be it.

He looked away from the smoldering shack. I think north is that way. But, then, on the other hand, it could be that-a-way, he looked 180-degrees. With no sunlight penetrating, and the uniform blanket of new whiteness covering any sign of tracks from last night, and the moss on the north side of the trees covered by four feet of snow, a heading was just a guess. Show me the way to go home. I'm tired and I want to go to bed, his right brain sang. Or maybe it's my left brain, he considered.

The snowmobile trail can't be too far away. Maybe a sled will come by and I'll hear it. On the other hand the woods of Wisconsin, inundated with snow, with more falling, were anechoic. Sound did not reverberate in the snowy woods he was stopping by. Wish I had a little horse to give the harness bells a shake, he thought.

Davecki shook his head. Focus, Dave. Focus.

Plot a transect and keep with it until I come to the sled trail, or a road, or, if by bad luck, the transect leads to Lake Superior's shore. If that happens I'll hole up under a balsam like a savvy whitetail and pass on to my greater reward. Or, better yet, head out on the ice and keep going to open water. Lake Superior doesn't give up its dead, you know. No body, no questions about what I was doing on Rez land. He thought of Davina, Stanski... even Seagull. Maybe Hawthorne will organize a little ceremony after I'm declared dead. They can stand around and talk in puns about me. He wiggled the heavy watch on his wrist. The thing seems destined to forever find deep water, I guess. Maybe Love is right about the curse.

Snap out of it, Dave. Remember the saying about a journey of ten thousand miles beginning with the first step. He wondered if Confucius was ever trapped in a blizzard with a mangled left foot. Daniel Day-Lewis had a left foot didn't he? Oh well, nothing to it but to do it, Davecki realized. He sighted down the side of two popple trees, taking measure of his intended trajectory and fixed his gaze on a third tree barely visible through the falling snow. He limped to what he hoped was south.

North was not good. There was nothing but brush and brush and trees and more trees to the north, to say nothing of even deeper lake effect snow. He took a painful step. Another. The snow was waist deep.

The urge to cry surged from his guts to his throat. This is bad, bad, bad, he thought.

One step at a time, the other side of his mind countered.

Not going to make it out of this one, Ma.

Inch by inch, his optimist countered.

It took five minutes to make it to the first sighting tree. He looked ahead. Which tree up there was my reference point? Huh. Could be any one of the four that looked sort of lined up. He looked back, saw his weaving, wobbly, uncertain groove in the snow that looked like a porcupine path. He'd made about twenty yards. He shook an inch of new snow off his shoulders.

This is bad.

He shook his head against defeat. He sighted back down his more-or-less straight track, turned 90 degrees and picked a tree twenty yards distant. Achievable goal…I think…he thought.

He took another step and the snow exploded in front of him and a little to his left. It was like a land mine going off as the grouse erupted like Vesuvius from under the pure white, smooth blanket of snow. "Lord, help me," Davecki yelled as he staggered backward. "Settle down, heart," he added as he watched the gliding brown blur of grouse slip-sliding away through the trees in the gray light and falling flakes. The bird tilted its wings this way and that, twisting and swerving in a graceful display of deep-woods navigation. That thing flies like Tom Cruise in Top Gun, he thought. Or, better yet, Luke Skywalker in an X-fighter.

Huffing from the scare, Davecki squelched another urge to cry. He stared through the millions, or even billions and billions of—thank you Carl Sagan, snowflakes surging down. "Lord, help me," he called out. He waded forward and stumbled. Face down in the snow, he did the breaststroke to clear the snow away and free his freezing face for breathing.

On all fours, head hung low in defeat, his bad side thought, this is badder than bad.

Yup, his good side agreed.

He didn't bother moving again. I'll just stay here and get buried. They'll find me in the spring. This isn't such a bad way to go, he thought. It's quiet. Serene. He shrugged his shoulders. Snow fell from them. He smiled weakly at the little dark spots where his involuntary tears made dark holes in the snow in front of his face. He recalled Dick Summers shooting an elk, gutting it, and crawling inside the warm body cavity to survive a high mountain blizzard. No elk for you, mon frère. His resistance at zero, his chest heaved and a choked sob blew out the block in his neck. Sobbing led to tears. Falling tears melted the snow in front of his face. Through watery eyes Davecki saw in the melting snow, a sliver of silver.

What in the world, he blinked.

Digging, digging, digging with mittened hands, the silver turned into a handle. The handle attached to a hatch cover. In an instant the despair turned into hope.

"Thank you, Lord," he muttered out loud.

Swishing and sweeping snow away, he levered the handle, pulling the round hatch door upwards. A gush of warm…compared-to-the-blizzard-around-him…air slapped his cheeks and insulted his aquiline nose. Darkness below. A set of descending ladder steps. A heavy duty industrial-looking toggle switch. Throw it. Light below.

Davecki looked heavenward, "Just like you, God, to put your answer right in front of my nose."

CHAPTER 18

Damaged foot and all, Davecki descended the ladder. Nine slow rungs later he looked up to the halo of darkness above. Cold fat snowflakes fell on his hot face. Should go back and close that hatch, he thought. Or not. My left foot hurts too much. *My Left Foot,* he thought of the movie. Christy Brown wouldn't let a little thing like a run-over foot stop him. I'm no Daniel Day-Lewis, Davecki thought, abandoning the urge to secure the hatch.

Taking in his new cozy tiny home he thought, not exactly Greenbrier, but way better than Bruce Beach's school busses and way, way better than freezing to death. The room was about twelve by twelve feet. Shelves lined the right wall. On said shelves, canned goods, boxes and stacks of paper goods. Must've stocked up before the pandemic, he thought. On the left, cupboards above a countertop. Cupboards below. Sink in the middle. Immediately left of the ladder, an incinerator toilet. A two-foot diameter table with two chairs in the center of the room, a Lindt chocolate bar sitting dead center. On the opposite wall, bunk beds. Somebody was planning for two, he thought.

He limped to the table, picked up the chocolate. Shouldn't, he thought. He put the temptation aside, limped to the counter. The faint aroma of rotten eggs. I'll take door number one, Wayne, he thought, opening a door below the counter. A bank of Trojan batteries.

Behind door number two above the counter, he found SpaghettiOs, Gimme Moore Stew, Spam, and Great Value Wild Atlantic Salmon in oil.

"Yum," he hummed, grabbing the canned salmon. A drawer yielded a can opener. Heat buildup under his arms provoked the disrobing of his Carhartt. The memory of a can-cut from his youth warned him away from fingering the salmon out in greedy, hunger-driven haste. Another drawer yielded a fork and the sharpness in his tummy quit complaining.

From his seat on the stainless-steel chair, with his elbows resting on the round table, he masticated the meat as he studied the pile of snow accumulating at the bottom of the ladder.

"You born in a barn or something?" he heard his mother's voice yelling at him when he neglected the little matter of closing the door upon entering or exiting as the case may be. It'd be a struggle to go up and close it, he thought, focusing back on his foot. Wonder who the idiot was that ran me over? Wonder what Harrison is up to right now, chasing around in the blizzard. Sucks to be him, Davecki thought, grinning. What's that guy up to with all these shenanigans, he wondered. Stealing a dog team, burning down a hunting cabin. Did he even burn it down? What's his motivation? Who's on second, he thought of Abbott and Costello. Where's Columbo when you need him?

Getting sleepy. I'm okay, he sent mental messages to Stanski and Hawthorne and Davina in Africa. He tipped the now empty can of salmon to his lips, wincing as he drank the oily fluid and flinching again at the thought of licking it out and cutting his tongue.

"I'll cut your tongue out, young man," he recalled his mother telling him after he'd repeated a swear word he'd heard.

"Thanks, Ma," he muttered. Clunking down the can, he leaned off the chair and tottered to the lower bunk, fell in, and, for the second time in very recent history, broke the cardinal rule of a broken foot: Never sleep with your boots on when your ankle is bruised or broken.

A body falling from the sky, thumping like a sack of potatoes to the floor, and finding voice with, "Arggh!" will wake up even the most exhausted deep sleeper.

Davecki shot up like an Asian Jumping Carp on the Mississippi, hit his head on the bunk above. "Arggh," he echoed, rubbing his head and looking at the mass of whatever on the floor across the bunker.

"Arggh," the mass across the floor responded.

Three argghs in under thirty seconds, Davecki thought. Must be a record, he thought, then he said, "What the?"

The bundle did Optimus Prime, transforming before Davecki's eyes from sack of potatoes to an upright, but sitting, human. "What the," Human Form asked, looking around.

Snow in volume flew from Human Form as he dusted himself off. Dark, weary eyes with drooping bags above an ice-encrusted black beard scanned the bunker, landing on Davecki.

"You again?" Harrison asked.

"I might say the same."

"Why don't you?"

Davecki rubbed his konked noggin again, said, "Because I'm curbing my enthusiasm for company dropping in."

The men eyed each other. Harrison remained seated in his pile of snow. He rubbed his right knee. Davecki ceased and desisted from massaging his head injury and lifted his Daniel Day-Lewis leg.

Man, I should have taken my boot off, he thought. "What's the weather like up there?"

Harrison decided the pile of snow was uncomfortable, got up, did the Wisconsin Winter Stomp, stamping each foot to free the snow. He walked to the table where Davecki's empty can of salmon lay. "Blizzard of the century," Harrison said.

"How come there's a blizzard of the century every winter?" Davecki asked.

Harrison sighed, picked up the can, "I'm starving. Any more of these?"

"Middle cupboard," Davecki said."

Harrison moved to the bank of cupboards, went through the same can opening routine.

The silence of the salmon engulfed the room. Anthony Hopkins and Jody Foster both would be unnerved. It did not rattle nerves-of-steel Alphonse "Dave" Davecki, who knew a thing or three about waiting out felons in tiny enclosed rooms. Interrogation rooms? Bunkers? Same, same. Plus, his left foot hurt and the throbs from the netherworld in his boot kept at least three of the compartments in his brain occupied.

Better hide the watch, Davecki thought. As Harrison scraped the bottom of the can Davecki took the Rolex off and stuffed it under the pillow. Watch tucked, he asked, "Would you be willing to help me get my boot off? It's all 'swolt' up," he said, harkening back to the Finnish accents he'd heard in the recent past while investigating a mysterious death on the Brule River.

Harrison jerked his sagging bearded head like a horse coming awake. Fork in hand, he studied Davecki.

Guy's fond of uncomfortable silence, Davecki thought.

Harrison took a last bite, said around the fish, "What happened to your foot?"

"Some fool snowmobiler ran it over after you nearly ran me down with the team. Speaking of which, where's Remington's team?"

"Oh, you mean *my* team?" Harrison said.

"What's that mean?"

Harrison plunked the can with its protruding fork on the table. He scraped the chair back and went to knee before Davecki. "It means all those dogs are Iditarod caliber dogs that I bred and raised over the last five years." He grabbed the heel and toe of Davecki's boot. "They're worth a fortune."

"Define fortune," Davecki asked.

"On average twenty-five grand apiece," he said as he pulled on the boot.

"Owie! Owie! Owie!" Davecki screeched.

Harrison looked at Davecki with wide eyes. "Big baby," he said, letting the foot down.

Sweat from the pain beading on his temples, Davecki asked, "That's a quarter-million-dollar team then?"

"Huh. You can multiply," Harrison answered, heading for the counter.

That takes care of motive, Davecki thought. "They okay up there?"

"The dogs are fine. Curled up and comfy no doubt."

Davecki moved his foot around, searching for relief.

Harrison peeled off his Carhartt, flung it over the nearest chair. He opened a drawer below the counter. Opening another drawer, he pulled out a long Old Hickory kitchen knife, held it up to the light, said, "Jack always liked good blades."

Returning, he said Davecki. "Give it up." He twitched the knife toward Davecki's left boot.

"Amputation so soon?"

"If that's what it takes, umm. Forgot your name."

"Some call me Dave," he refrained from adding, The Enchanter. Lifting Daniel Day-Lewis to the knife wielder's right hand, he added, "Alphonse "Dave" Davecki."

Harrison raised his eyes from the boot in question to Davecki's face. "You know your initials stand for Attention Deficit Disorder, don't you?"

"Never occurred to me." Guess even bad guys have a little good in them, he thought.

Harrison twisted the knife this way and that, commenced to cutting laces. They popped aside like worms cut in half for the hook. "Nice," Harrison said.

"You're a knife man?" Davecki asked.

"That was Jack's style. I'm a gun guy. Knives are too up close and personal," Harrison said.

Small comfort, Davecki thought.

The operation was ugly in so many ways. Destroying a beautifully made $150 dollar boot. Well, actually destroying one $75 boot. Then there was the pain, through which Davecki winced and twitched and yelped.

"Suck it up, Dave. Your whining is bugging me and you don't want to make me mad."

"You Lou Ferrigno or something?" Davecki asked.

"Humpf," the knifeman answered as he cut the last of the boot free. He sliced away the yellow and black hand-knit heavy wool sock Davina made for his Christmas present last year. "There you go," he said. He set the captive foot free and returned to the salmon can.

Gonna be a blue blue Christmas without you, boot, Davecki thought. Davina will have more knitting now. He said, "That feels way better." He bent down to rub his black and blue foot. Doesn't look too bad, he thought.

Harrison said around the protein in his mouth, "This stuff sucks. I'm used to fresh salmon straight out of the ocean. Wonder if there's any Kind bars here, those things are good."

"There's a chocolate bar right in front of you."

"Can't eat that stuff. Hives, cramps and bloating to boot," he said, glancing at the pile of boot shards on the floor. "Now, a Kind bar. That would be awesome. Carczak loved those things." He forked in more salmon.

"Speaking of Carczak, what happened to him in Alaska?"

"They say a bear got him. Or he fell and died, or got lost and starved. Or he met up with some mean ugly hikers and made them mad."

Davecki studied Harrison's face. It was round and bearded and grizzled with deep lines radiating from the corners of the eyes so blue. White shards of melting ice clung to the foot-long straggles of hair descending from under a fur hat. If there was an aura there, it radiated craft and deceit and oozed a little slime. "Sounds like it might have been you that he made mad up there."

"Me? No way, Jose. Jack was a jerk," Harrison said, scraping the bottom of the can with his fork. "But I didn't kill him."

He's lying, Davecki thought.

Harrison set the can down, sighed, burped, and went to the cupboard in the corner. "Gotta be some Kind bars here somewhere." He opened the cupboard door nearest the corner, paused for a few moments looking up like a collie waiting for its master to toss down a treat. Then, "That son of a bitch! I knew it. I just knew it."

Davecki couldn't see what Harrison was staring at. He got off his bunk, hobbled to Harrison's side. "Holy mackerel!"

The men stood transfixed.

Harrison's head bobbed as if counting.

Davecki reached out a trembling hand that proved his nerves of steel were more like wiggling worms just now. Felons in custody? No problem. Multiple fatal car crash? Coronavirus pandemic? No problems.

This?

Serious anxiety.

He grabbed a quart jar from the shelf, pulled it away, said, "Holy mackerel, this is heavy."

"Don't drop that."

Harrison reached up and grabbed his own quart jar. He moved

his hand deep into the cupboard. "Four ranks deep. Six across, times four shelves."

"Holy mackerel!" Davecki said.

"That's 24 bottles per shelf, times four," Harrison said.

"Holy mackerel!"

"Stop saying that!"

"Sorry. Sorry."

"I'd say around six million. Just a rough estimate," Harrison said.

Guy must be a math whiz, Davecki thought. "You can tell just by looking?" Davecki asked, lifting his quart jar toward the light bulb above.

The gold in the jar glittered.

"Yeah, plus I've been chasing this around for years now. I knew he hit it big in Nome. He was the first guy to suction dredge offshore. Built a gigantic wheeled dredge from an old LeTourneau Arctic Train. Complete with a huge aluminum sluice box on top. He wandered around offshore sucking up black sand. Plus, I know a thing or three about the price of gold. It's never been far from my mind for fifteen years. Guess I burned the hunting shack down for nothing."

Hefting the quart jar of gold, Davecki thought, arsonist, murderer, dog team thief, *and* a gold expert? Quite a guy. At least now the Rolex makes sense. Carczak could afford it. "There's that much gold in them thar hills?" Davecki asked.

"All you gotta do is find good pay," Harrison said. "He had a Lamborghini and a pricy girlfriend at his house in Switzerland," Harrison said.

"Did it burn down too?"

"Wouldn't surprise me," Harrison said.

"How much gold can a miner get?" Davecki asked. "Seems like a lot." He put the jar back on the shelf.

"It all depends on the dirt, man. You get good pay, the sky's the limit."

Feeling a little dizzy, Davecki hobbled back to his bunk. Sitting, he rubbed his banged-up cranium. He felt a combination of brain freeze, the tipsy whirl of an alcoholic buzz, and the feeling of waking up after being knocked cold by Barry Pirkola's wild pitch in high school. All that gold, in a survivalist bunker, in the middle of the woods of Hayfield County, in somebody else's name…makes me dizzy, Davecki thought.

CHAPTER 19

Thinking of the sky above, Davecki glanced over to the bunker's landing zone where Harrison had fallen from the sky like manna from heaven. Well, not exactly manna, he thought. A-mana? But he's not from Iowa. More like Satan the fallen angel. The snow he expected to see coming down the entrance tube was AWOL. Must have drifted over, he thought. Or the blizzard quit. Then he thought, how is this going to end?

His worthy opponent opened the cupboard next to the gold. "Hmm," he said, "Jack did favor peanut butter and cheese crackers."

Watching Harrison pull a carton of crackers from the shelf, Davecki thought, okay. One question at a time. That's the way to do it. Your money for nothing and your answers for free. "Why did you say the dog team was yours?"

Returning to the round table, Harrison glanced at his worthy opponent, answered, "None of your beeswax, nosy."

Is he a second grader, Davecki wondered, as Harrison struggled with thick fumbling fingers to free at last the crackers from the cellophane. "Dang things," he said. "I'm too hot." He tossed the crackers down. Standing, he undid the front of his Carhartt bibs, let the flap fall. He sat, plucked the nutrition from the table and recommenced his struggle against the hegemony of plastic. "It's a long story," the calorie seeker said, putting teeth to cellophane and ripping open the recalcitrant package.

"We've got time," Davecki said, eyeing the entrance again. "Gotta be a heckuva dump going on up there."

Harrison didn't answer. He stuffed peanut butter crackers into his maw like a hungry dog gobbling tasty Redpaw.

Watching the man masticate, Davecki felt hungry too. He slipped off the bunk, put his good foot forward, shook his bad foot all about, hobbled the short distance to the crackers on the table, grabbed a packet of energy, and commenced to implement his own strategy for feeding himself. He pinched the corner of the packet with thumb and forefinger and ripped. Munching the tasty morsel, Davecki asked, "How'd you find this, anyway?"

This question Harrison was willing to answer. "Didn't." He wiggled another cracker sandwich from the packet. Before opening mouth and inserting food, he added, "Dogs found it. I was totally lost in the blizzard. Really a mess out there. Reminds me of the Halloween blizzard back in '91. Anyway, I just hung on as the dogs plowed snow. Knew they couldn't last much longer and when they stopped, I took one step off the runners and fell down here. Dogs knew what they were doing."

Davecki lifted cracker to mouth, studied it, "And Carczak? He's responsible for this?" Insert cracker. "Nom. Nom."

The dog thief flicked a weary glance at Davecki, said, "I'm bushed. Got to get some sleep." He got up and approached the bunk beds, "Short version is," he said as he climbed to the top bunk, "after we ditched Vegas for Alaska, we went prospecting north of Fairbanks. I got sick of mining and took off. Then the lucky bastard hit a huge pay streak. Then he went to Nome and did even better. My share of the proceeds, among other things, is what I've been chasing ever since."

The bedsprings above Davecki squawked in complaint as gravity and the heavy body applied pressure.

Among other things? What's that mean? Maybe he knows about the watch. Got to conceal it better after he falls asleep. "But didn't you quit the claim before he struck gold?"

"My name is still on the claim papers," the voice bounced off the black ash tongue and groove ceiling above.

"And he never shared?"

"Ha! Jack Carczak share?"

Following a short silence from above, little snores fell. Davecki pondered an escape plan. With Daniel Day-Lewis foot hobbling him, scrambling up the tunnel of not love was feasible. Better get some sleep too, he thought.

The snoring changed tune. It was loud enough to register on the Richter Scale in Golden, Colorado or at least settle the snow above the bunker.

No sleep for you, Davecki. He took a pillow. Wrapped it around his head. Man, this is weird. I wonder what Stanski's doing? Rescuing stranded motorists, no doubt. Or completely snowed in. How much of what Harrison said is true? He studied the cabinet doors with six million dollars' worth of gold behind. The next to the last thing he thought as the lights in the bunker automatically extinguished was, huh, motion detector.

Then he thought, Lord help me.

CHAPTER 20

The next morning, noon, or night—depending on how long Davecki slept—came when he woke to the smell of bacon. Bacon in a bunker? I don't recall seeing a refrigerator, he thought. Terrible draw on the batteries, he thought. I wonder where the generator is? Is there an escape tunnel? Consider the mouse and all that. Then he opened his eyes. The first thing he saw was the serious looking 1911 style pistol resting comfortably in the middle of the round table. Looks 9mm from the size of the muzzle, Davecki thought. Beside the weapon of not mass destruction…more weaponry in the form of a pile of plastic sporks. Harrison faced the counter. One of his Carhartt suspender straps dangled toward the floor. Davecki sniffed. "Bacon?" he asked as he swung his feet out, Daniel Day-Lewis protesting wildly against the movement.

"Bacon bits," Harrison answered without turning. "Jack had a thing for bacon."

"Don't we all?"

"I suppose. But Jack was obsessed."

"Sounds like you guys were close," Davecki said, thinking of Stanski.

"Yeah, until the S.O.B. double-crossed me."

It'd be great if Stan showed up suddenly, he thought.

Davecki peered around Harrison to see what he was chopping. "But you quit the mine before the strike."

"So? We split a hundred and fifty bucks in Vegas on our way to Alaska. He lost his half. I won sixteen grand. We..." he emphasized the "we" with a drawn-out tightness in his voice, "... used that money to file the claims." Harrison swept chunks of dehydrated orange mango into an already existing heap of canned salmon chunks and bacon bits. "Now it's all mine," he said.

Davecki opened a cupboard door, pulled two Melmac plates out. "What about Kitty Love? As his daughter she's the rightful heir." He handed said Melmac to Harrison.

"Hah!" Harrison laughed. "She's not his daughter and she knows it. She's just playing the part. Everybody assumes she's his kid. But I know different."

Davecki knew a thing or two about spaghetti lives. He'd been involved with tangled messes and woeful tragedies his entire career. Just when one thing gets figured out, ten more complications arise from the muddy water of past histories, infidelities, crimes and passions. They sneak up on the unsuspecting, unprepared and unwitting with their unbelievable lyrics, sing the blues, mess with the mind, and make fiction look like child's play. He took the plate Harrison returned with food heaped, hobbled back to the table. "So, don't leave me hanging, Harrison."

"Call me Harry," Harrison said as he beat the cripple to the table. Sitting he said, "Kitty's my kid," he said. He shoved the 1911 to the side, picked up a spork and scooped breakfast of not-champions.

Sitting, Davecki thought, oh what tangled webs we weave. "Seriously?" he asked. He sporked some bacon-mango-salmon in. Yuk, he thought but recalled his number one culinary rule, never complain to the cook, curbing his enthusiasm to speak badly of what God hath provided. Plus, the cook was well armed.

Before taking his next bite, Harrison said, "She'll deny it, but Molly told me the truth and I knew anyway because Jack was in jail when we had sex."

So, who's the piker now, Davecki thought. He wished he had his Columbo notebook to write all this stuff down. He tried to envision a piece of paper in his head with the family tree diagram on it, but only managed to see a wispy form of white, like a cloud or a puff of hot breath in the cold air above. Wonder how the dogs are doing, he thought. "So you and Molly were having an affair while Carczak was in jail and then you and he took off for Alaska."

Harrison swallowed, flicked eyes at Davecki, "Something like that. You writing a book or something? What you doing out here on the Rez anyway?"

Davecki, always a believer in transparency, even though it often came back to bite him, answered, "I used to be a cop and I came out here looking for you at the request of my former partner, who's a Hayfield County deputy, who, in the line of duty, was trying to recover an allegedly stolen dog team."

Harrison hard-swallowed a mouthful of salmon-bacon-mango delight.

Davecki saw the news was going down hard as the nutrition.

"Shit," Harrison said. "Should've known." He pulled the 1911 closer to his edge of the table. "You just play your cards cool, old man and you'll be just fine. Don't go making me do anything worth regretting."

Davecki's nerve endings that had earlier been mushy hot noodles, stiffened up under threat of threat. "I'm retired, Harry. I'll let the Feds take care of this business."

"Feds?"

"Tribal lands are under the jurisdiction of the FBI. That's why Stanski asked me to go for a stroll where local law enforcement needs permission to go."

"Frikkin' Carczak. He always said being half Indian was the best thing that ever happened to him."

"He was Native?"

"You Captain Obvious or something?" Harrison reached over, picked up Davecki's empty Melmac, stacking it on top of his. He picked up the gun and stuffed it between his bulging belly and Carhartt bib before walking to the counter and putting the plates in a plastic tub.

"Chippewa?"

"It's Ojibwe now, dummy. His ma was Ojibwe," Harrison said, as he walked to the cupboard containing the mother lode. He opened the doors. Harrison hung there, gazing at the fortune in gold.

Davecki moved to his bunk. Harrison said, "This much weighs around 3,000 pounds. Way too much for the team to carry out in one trip."

Captain Obvious realized Harrison couldn't leave a witness to six mil in undeclared gold. Lord, help me, he prayed. He studied Harrison's profile. A big man. Probably 240 or 250 with that belly. With this foot, I'll lose in a fight.

Harrison let go the doors, started pulling drawers.

He's going to shoot me outside, Davecki realized. The wolves rampant in Hayfield County will smell the blood and dispose of the body. That 9mm is going to make a mess of my head.

"Nice," Harrison said, lifting a spool of paracord from a drawer.

Wonder if I could get the gun away from him. Probably not with Daniel Day-Lewis making me nimble as a porcupine. But better odds than a wrestling match.

"Get off your butt and bring me a blanket," Harrison said.

Davecki complied. Maybe I can grab the gun.

"Spread it out," Harrison said, grabbing a corner and backing away.

So much for that plan, Davecki thought.

Harrison pulled down a jar. "Pillowcase," he nodded.

Davecki limped to obey.

"Each one of these is worth about 60-grand," Harrison said as they wrapped more jars. "I'll take twenty now." He paused again. Scratched the back of his head. "That'll be 600 pounds. Too heavy for the dogs in this snow. Ten will do. That'll be 600K. I'll be able to buy a helicopter and come back for the rest."

"You fly helicopters?"

He dragged the gold-laden blanket to the ladder, toeing what was left of the melting snow aside. "Why do you think I went nuts in the first place? Uncle Sam made me a warrant officer. Sent me to Nam. Normal people don't get bat-shit crazy unless they are given the privilege and option to kill and or die for their country. Ever hear of a poet named Wilfred Owen?"

"Can't say that I have."

"World War One poet. Dulce et decorum est. It is sweet and fitting to die for one's country."

"Seriously?"

"Or…slaughter innocents from above with dual fifty cals for their country."

Ouch, Davecki thought.

"And have peaceniks spit on you in the airport."

Double ouch, Davecki thought.

"Then that bastard Nixon…."

Lotta vets came back and didn't go nuts, Davecki thought.

"Ford wasn't any better."

But then, not all vets flew Hueys and Cobras, Davecki thought.

"You're going to help haul this up," Harrison said.

Using the paracord he tied the corners of the blanket into a sling.

"And give me a chance to escape?"

"Not with that foot and the snow," Harrison said. He patted the black butt of the gun protruding from the tan flap of his bibs.

"Up you go."

Time for pleasantries is coming to an end, Davecki realized, moving toward the ladder.

Snow cascaded down on his face as he punched up with his left hand while clinging to the top rung of the ladder. Seeing the bare wrist where the watch used to be, he was glad he'd buried it deep in the pocket of his pants under his Carhartt bibs. His bare left foot pounded in pain as he pounded on the snow roof. Maybe I can rouse the team and make a fast getaway before he gets up the ladder.

Quit grasping at straws, Alphonse. The dogs won't know what's going on. The snow will be too deep. Maybe Stanski, the Tribal Police, the Feds, and Cousin Longmire will be up top waiting for Punxsutawney Phil and his pal to appear.

Or not.

Maybe I should kick him in the face when he pops out. Make a run for it.

Or not.

Then. Daylight. Bright, sunny, blinding daylight.

Davecki clung to the top rung, clearing snow with one hand. The white stuff seemed unending. He packed and pushed and dragged himself out.

Harrison was right behind him.

So much for shutting him in, Davecki thought.

Like magic a dog's black nose appeared in the world of white. Then blinking eyes and a pink tongue licking black lips. White fangs and a pretty-boy smile. Time for true religion that will bring you to your knees, if you please.

White Fang. Jack London genius, Davecki thought.

The dog, maybe it was Rivka, or possibly Regal, some R name for sure, stood and shook its snow-covered coat. Davecki grabbed the mainline and scooted himself aside as Harrison threw a blanket out ahead of him and emerged, rope in hand.

Rolling onto his back, sputtering snow from his mouth and

wiping the frosty white covering from his face, Davecki made another roll and bumped into another something solid. The something solid moved and another mound of snow transformed into a sled dog. The dog got up slowly, like it had been run hard and put away wet. Thank you Dan Rather, Davecki thought. The dog shook itself off, spraying snow into Davecki's face again.

"Thanks a lot, buddy," Davecki said, wiping snow away.

"That's Rascal," Harrison's voice came from behind. "Here," he handed Davecki a shank of rope. "Go easy, don't want any jars breaking."

The men pulled, easing the sling upwards. It bumped over each ladder rung with a muffled clink and tink of glass jars swaddled in blanket and pillowcase. Daniel kept up a constant complaint. Wish I had that boot back, Davecki thought.

"Easy, man." Harrison cautioned. He looked around as they pulled. "Man. Heckuva dump. Three more feet at least."

His voice had the weird anechoic quality of speech in an echoless chamber. Reminds me of John Cage's four-thirty-three, Davecki thought. Every limb, every tree trunk, the outhouse, the sled…everything was covered in snow. The sky was bright blue and cloudless above the snow-covered witch-finger tree limbs wearing their snowy white gloves. The calm after the storm before the storm of getting out of this alive, Davecki thought.

"Warmed up nice," Harrison said, a bead of sweat on his hairy temple.

With the sling out of the bunker, Harrison said, "Move away." Davecki plowed snow scooting backwards. Harrison shook the sled free of snow. The team, getting the message, all stood and shook and stretched. Slogging in the deep snow Harrison swung the sled around and unzipped the basket bag. As he undid the blanket sling the team got itself motivated. A growl here. A yawn there. Some jaw snapping and teeth clacking.

I should tackle him, Davecki thought. He tried to stand. The snow was like quicksand.

Harrison pulled jar after jar out of the sling, transferring them to the sled and tucking each in the inside blanket. "Be a total mess if one of these breaks on the way out," he said, turning his back to get another jar.

Quick as he could, Davecki dove, grabbed the sled runner and heaved it toward Harrison.

The sound of breaking glass. "Arrgh!" Harrison hollered as the sled landed on top of him.

The crash of glass and the jerk of the sled spooked the dogs. They took off as if they were bringing serum to Nome for the diphtheria epidemic.

"Go! Go! Go!" Davecki yelled as he and Daniel hobbled after.

Harrison floundered like a whale out of water as Team Davecki lurched away.

"Go! Go! Go!" Davecki yelled.

The dogs jumped and clawed and pulled, surging away.

Davecki caught up to the sled. Pushing on the bow, he churned away with utter disregard for his left foot until said foot struck something hard under the snow. He instantly lost his footing and fell. In that instant a gunshot erupted. Wood flew as the sled bow shattered. Snow cascaded from tree limbs above as the shock wave passed. It was as if a second blizzard had suddenly started.

Face down on all fours again, Davecki skipped sad donkey for scrambling cat clawing along the path the team made. Lungs burning in pain from the adrenaline rush combined with Daniel Day-Lewis screaming an Oscar-worthy performance in intense protest, Davecki prayed, Lord, help me.

Despite the sound-deadening effect of the snow, another "BANG" sounded behind.

That's two, Davecki counted as he churned through the snow.

Seven shot clip most likely, he thought when no more gunshots rang out.

Run Lola Run, he thought of the French film. More like crawl Davecki crawl!

Then a miracle. Packed down snow. He looked past the team lined out on the snowmobile trail. Beyond the team a couple of hundred yards, the backside of the Hayfield County Snow Bunny's trail groomer heading south. "Stop!" he yelled to no avail as the machine kept going. Lurching toward the sled, he realized, I'm too old for this.

CHAPTER 21

At the sled, Davecki looked down. So odd seeing one booted foot, one bare foot. Daniel felt dead. Davecki wiggled toes. Only they didn't wiggle. No feeling there. About halfway up his calf, there was some vague tingly feeling, but the foot? Nada. Probably going to lose that foot, he thought.

"BANG!" another shot rang out.

That's three, Davecki thought, looking back through the trees. Harrison stood, taking aim for another shot.

"GO! GO! GO!" he hollered.

The team launched, Davecki ducked and grabbed at the shattered bow as the slug whizzed past.

Yells from behind.

Who's a good dog? Davecki thought. Me. I am. I'm a good dog.

The woods rolled past like a newsreel. Tears rushed after one another as the water flowed from his eyes out and down his cheeks.

Gonna make it, he thought. "Whoo hooo!" he yelled.

At the yell, the team stopped. The sled slammed into the wheel dogs. Davecki did an ugly somersault over the handle and landed on top of the basket. More pain in his butt.

Rampart looked back with a face that said, "What in the world is wrong now?"

Davecki shook the sled forth and back as the wheel dogs reorganized themselves, casting disgusted looks at yet another musher confusing them.

"GO!" Davecki yelled.

Rampart shook his head, gave a look that said, "Make up your mind, will you please?" And the team took off running.

Bouncing along in the basket, Davecki shifted this way and that, hearing the crunch of broken glass beneath his bleeding butt. He held on with both hands and moved to the side until the pain lessened. The rhythm of the ride organized into something resembling routine. He reached between his legs, spread the basket bag open, plucked up a jar and heaved it as far off the trail as he could. Running down the road trying to lighten my load, he thought, lifting Daniel and extracting another jar. "Owie!" he yelped as a shard of glass cut his finger. Extracting another jar that had shiny shards of glass and brilliant flecks coating it, he yelled, "Sayonara," and heaved.

POOF, the jar splashed into the deep snow well off the side of the trail.

Somewhere far behind, perhaps in a galaxy far away, something went bang and pop.

CHAPTER 22

This is a warm, pleasant dream, Davecki thought.

The beautiful oval face of Brekken Hawthorne hovered above him like an angel floating in the blue sky above. Why is my belly doing flip-flops?

"You're a total mess, Dave. Bleeding from the hand and butt and a grazing head wound, but you're going to be fine."

"Sweet," he mumbled.

"What'd he say?" Stanski's rough voice asked.

The warm fuzzies turned cold icies when Stanski's voice intruded and Angel Hawthorne's visage vanished. All-business-Stan's voice said, "No sign of Harrison. Snow sled tracks on top of dog team tracks. Musta gotten a ride. Leapthorn is on it."

Come back, Brekken. Leapthorn? The Tribal Police guy? Is this heaven? Why is my brain so foggy? Why does my left foot hurt so bad? Why is my back so cold?

"Harrison's slippery as an eel," Hawthorne's voice drifted in from stage left. "Who knows? Might even have a pal or two we don't know about."

"He's stabilized," a woman's voice came in stage right.

"Thanks, Elisabeth," another male voice chimed in. "Good to transfer?"

"Yup," Elisabeth's voice answered.

Maybe I'm dead, Davecki thought. But shouldn't I be hovering above, seeing all, knowing all, feeling euphoric and torn between heading to the light or returning to my body?

The world shook as movement vibrated up his tender backside and all along the bricks in the wall. Hey teacher, leave those kids alone. Warmer. My back feels warmer now.

"That foot looks real bad," Elisabeth said. "Probably going to lose it."

"Hey! I'm right here!" Davecki yelled.

"What's he saying?" Hawthorne's voice asked.

"He's whispering something," Stanski said.

"Dilaudid's kicking in," Elisabeth answered.

"You gave him d-lala?" Hawthorne asked.

"Just what the doctor ordered," Elisabeth answered.

"He's going to love that," Stanski said. "Thanks for coming up so quick, Brekken. I'm heading to the station. Call me if he's dying or something else minor."

"Your concern is underwhelming," Hawthorne said.

"One-two-three," sounded clearly. One voice to rule them all. Davecki's stomach lurched at the feeling of flying.

Big-time bumping and banging around. "I'll ride with him," Hawthorne said, followed by the sound of slamming doors.

Davecki wondered, where's my truck? A high-pitched whining sound. That sucks, Davecki thought. The whining turned into thumping. The thumping turned into rocking. The feeling of being rocked to sleep. Don't fall asleep, Dave, he admonished himself. That's the cardinal rule of winter survival.

Sudden fear. "Don't amputate," he yelled.

Brekken voice, "What'd he say?"

"Don't know. He's whispering. Pretty doped up. Won't

remember a thing," Elisabeth answered.

Brekken asked, "Why are his eyes so glazed looking?"

"Stupefaction stare," Elisabeth replied.

Makes sense, Davecki thought. I am pretty stupid.

Hawthorne's gorgeous face appeared as if by magic, but this time it seemed as if it was a million miles away and hovering in a sky of silver. "You'll be fine, Dave."

"I love you, Brekken," he did declare.

"I can't hear you. Speak up."

He yelled as loud as he could, "Will you marry me, Brekken?"

"Wish I could understand him," Hawthorne said.

"That d-lala is good stuff," Elisabeth's voice came from far away.

Eyes blurred. Sleep. Like shutting down Hal in *2001*.

The sweet smell of a lovely woman wafted to his nose as the blur of Brekken's ear brushed his nose. "What? What?" she asked.

He had to get it out before astronaut Dave pulled out the last of Hal's personality cards. "Will you marry me?" Davecki bellowed.

"Isn't that something?" Hawthorne said. "I think he just whispered a proposal in my ear."

"Like I said, that d-lala is good," Elisabeth laughed. "Only trouble is he won't remember that he popped the question in a helicopter after narrowly escaping death."

"Of course I'll marry you, Dave. But only if you have a lot of money," Hawthorne answered. Her pretty lips curved into a teasing smile. Her green eyes twinkled with delight and spunk and devilishness.

Sweet, Davecki thought. Davina will be pleased. I'll go back in the spring and fetch me a bunch of gold-filled jars.

"Harrison?" he asked.

"Short honeymoon," Hawthorne laughed, added, "He's on the run again. We've been trying to pin something on him for years, ever since he killed Carczak in Alaska."

"Huh?" He wanted to sit up and get things organized. Ask questions worthy of Columbo, like who's on second, but he felt all dreamy and mushy and like his body was all water, no flesh and bones. Plus there was the pesky noise and vibration of helicopter flight. No wonder warrant officers went bonkers, he thought.

"Long story, Alphonse. Don't fret about it. I'm on the case now that federal jurisdiction is in play."

"Carczak murdered?"

"We think so. Case is real cold, though. Don't bother about it. We've got it covered. Just focus on getting well."

Davecki wiggled his wrist, wanted to feel the reassuring weight of his future with Hawthorne. No weighty-weight there. Oh no! Lost again. So much for getting married at Skid May's Ledges, he thought. That'll never happen with the watch gone. I feel drunk. Feels good. Like I knew it would. He raised his watch arm, waved it all about.

"What? What?" Elisabeth asked.

"More," Davecki mumbled.

"Huh?"

"D-lala land," Davecki mangled his request.

"You're well dosed already, sir."

"Shucks," Davecki said. I do feel good, he thought. "Like I knew I would," he sang.

Elisabeth and Hawthorne grinned at one another.

"All the gold in Hayfield County is in a bunker in the middle of the woods in Hayfield County in somebody else's name," Davecki sang.

"He's no Larry Gatlin," Hawthorne said.

"You were always on my mind. You were always on my mind," Davecki switched to Elvis.

"His voice isn't that bad," Elisabeth said.

The voices beside him laughed. But they were getting far away. Further away. He fell farther in, relishing the drug-induced euphoria with no thought of the anguish to come.

CHAPTER 23

"My mother used to say, 'When the booze goes in, the truth comes out,'" Brekken Hawthorne said.

"A wise woman," Stanski said.

In the silence that followed, Davecki felt as if the block of ice he was frozen in melted more slowly than the Ross Ice Shelf under threat of climate change. Where am I? What are Stanski and Hawthorne talking about? Who's on first? Wait a second, wasn't there a third party involved? Where's Columbo's notebook?

"I wonder if they gave him OxyContin?" Stanski asked.

"Dilaudid," Hawthorne said.

"I hear that's some sweet stuff," Stanski said.

Oh. Yeah, I'm not dead, Davecki realized. Just doped up. Then it occurred to him to look at the pain thing that was happening way down south beyond New Orleans. It was like looking through binoculars backwards. There was a burning sensation far, far away. Something like a burning shack in the deep woods of the Reservation where there was also an Archie Bunker of gold. Or maybe it was further away, Moses and the burning bush distance. Maybe it should be farther away. Farther along we'll know all about it. Farther along we'll understand why. So cheer up my brothers, live in the sunshine. We'll understand this, all by and by.

He shook his wrist. Nothing.

"He's coming out of it, I think," Hawthorne said.

"Yup. A little at least," Stanski said.

I wonder if they know about the Archie Bunker of gold, Davecki thought. "What's Archie's story?" he heard himself say.

"Huh?" Stanski asked.

"It's the drug talking," Hawthorne said.

"Or drugs," Stanski added.

Okay brain, Davecki thought, straighten out and think right, er, no, left, er correctly. "You know, Archie Bunker," came out of his mouth that suddenly felt dry, his tongue the size and texture of a balled-up wad of paper toweling. Not that he'd ever stuck a wad of paper toweling in his mouth to stop the flow of blood from losing that molar in that fist fight in north Oulu that Summer Solstice Juhannus Festival night outside the Cultural Center that Jack and Diane built in the back of the Chevy on the way to the levy.

Oh, please, please Bahrain stop being so muddled.

"I bet he's thinking about Harrison's survivalist bunker," Hawthorne said.

"I bet," Stanski agreed.

I'm right here, Davecki thought. And, it was Carczak's bunker by the way.

Some part of his brain that had managed to avoid the d-lala wash suggested…it might help if you open your eyes.

Hey, that's not a bad idea, some other compartment in Davecki's segmented brain agreed. Okay, eyes, do your thing, he thought, or at least one part of his brain thought. Maybe I'm

Multiple Personality Disorder, a different segment thought. MPD instead of A.D.D. Deputy Alphonse Dave Davecki reporting for duty.

Okay, eyes, get with it.

The ayes have it.

Hawthorne and Stanski popped into view, each to either side of the hospital bed and all the brain-chaff-noise-ticker-tape-parade-of-cascading-thoughts fell away and into the abyss where they belonged.

"Wow," Davecki said, "I'm really thirsty."

"Welcome back, buddy," Stanski said.

Hawthorne picked up the climate-change-contributing Styrofoam cup complete with super offensive plastic straw on the rolling nightstand, moving it to Davecki's lips.

"Thanks, I can do it." He reached for the cup.

"Not with that bandaged hand," Hawthorne said. She stuck the straw toward his chapped lips.

Cool, clear, water, he thought. Thank you Marty Robbins. Man, am I whacked, he thought.

"That tastes sooo good," he said. Smacking his lips, he wished he had some toasted bread soaked through with butter and maple syrup and covered in cinnamon. "How long I been out?"

Stanski pulled the nightstand drawer open, retrieved the two-million-dollar watch, studied it briefly, "It's almost noon, so I'd say about twenty hours."

Davecki looked at the watch, then at Stanski, then at Hawthorne, then back to the water cup, if that thing is worth so much, maybe I should ask her out. Stanski would be miffed though. With his outside voice, he asked, "Harrison in custody?"

"Not yet," Hawthorne said. She looked out the window that faced the mighty expanse of frozen Lake Superior.

Baby, it's cold outside, Davecki thought. Her eyes are like starlight, he recalled one line from the song.

"What happened?"

"After the blizzard blew over, everyone and their aunts, uncles, nephews, and cousins started looking for you. Willie Scott saved the tribal police, two counties, and the state Mounties a ton of money by calling in from the groomer that he'd found the team and you half dead with only one boot on," Stanski said.

Boot Hill. Here lies Les Moore, four slugs from a .44, some pesky Bahrain brain compartment shot out.

Settle down, brain, Davecki commanded.

"Harrison managed to nearly blow your stupid head off," Stanski added.

Hawthorne glared at Stanski, added, "Harrison managed to get an undetermined number of quart jars filled with placer gold gone. Know anything about that, Alphonse?"

"He said there was six million or so. That it all belonged to him. That he deserved it," Davecki answered.

"It'll RICO up nicely," Stanski said.

Hawthorne scowled at Stanski again, went on, "He jacked an Arctic Cat from a guy named Erik from Merrill and made it to Cornucopia. Bugs me bad that I haven't caught him."

"He's a slippy one," Davecki said.

"Slippy?" she asked, finally looking at him.

"It's Canadian for elusive as hell," Stanski interpreted.

"Tell me about it," she said, lowering her chin and shaking her head a little.

Stanski took up the narrative. "In Corny he stole a Lexus from a woman named Trixie and vanished."

"The Lexus turned up in Grandview yesterday evening where the trail went cold."

I wonder if my watch will be RICOed, Davecki thought.

A nurse in pale green scrubs and wearing a mask entered and walked to the foot of Davecki's bed.

"Elisabeth. Nice to see you," Hawthorne said.

"Hi, Brekken. Good, he's awake. He remember anything from our flight in?" Elisabeth asked. The mask hid most hints at the nurse's age, but her voice conveyed youth and enthusiasm.

"What? What?" Davecki asked.

"Guess not," Hawthorne said.

"Too bad," Elisabeth said. "I'll alert Doctor Ami."

"What's that all about?" Davecki asked.

"Nothing. You were talking crazy talk on the Life Flight here," Hawthorne said.

"Like what?" Davecki asked.

"You were singing Larry Gatlin and Elvis songs," Hawthorne said.

"He was?" Stanski asked.

"I was?" Davecki asked.

"Among other things," Hawthorne said.

"Like what?" Davecki asked.

"You threw a little James Brown in too."

"Me singing?"

"I've never ever heard him sing," Stanski said.

"If you don't believe it, ask nurse Elisabeth," Hawthorne said.

Right on cue, said nurse and a dark-haired woman with the stereotypical stethoscope dangling around her neck entered.

"Was he singing on the flight in?" Stanski asked.

"He was. Nice voice," Elisabeth said.

"That's a first," Stanski said.

"What's the word, Doc?" Hawthorne asked.

"He's a tough old badger," the doctor answered. Her black long hair emphasized an oval face with curvaceous lips and piercing eyes. "No amputation today."

"Sweet," Davecki said.

"Awesome," Stanski said.

"Tough and lucky," Hawthorne added.

The health care duo moved to the bedside as Stanski and

Hawthorne stepped back. The doctor grabbed Davecki's Rolexless wrist. She twisted the arm attached to that wrist and bent close to the IV extruding from his flesh. "Looking good," she said, donning the stethoscope and plunking the cold disk to the bare skin between his neck and gown.

"Geez, Doc. That thing's cold!"

"My heart bleeds for you, sir," the doctor said.

Stanski guffawed.

Hawthorne snickered.

Dr. Ami removed the stethoscope. "I'd expect a man of your age to have at least a little congestion after an ordeal like that." She smiled. "Okay, let's have a look at your backside."

"No way," Davecki said.

"Way," the doctor ordered. "Your friends can leave the room now."

"No way," Stanski said.

"I'm outta here," Hawthorne said, heading for the door.

"OUT!" Doctor Ami nodded at Stanski who shuffled toward the door. "Over you go," she said, lifting the covers.

Davecki rolled right. Cold air smacked his back.

"Looks a little better already," Dr. Ami said.

"I agree," Elisabeth said.

Hawthorne and Stanski returned as the medical professionals exited.

Around the bed again, naturally, Davecki asked, "So. How we going to hang Harry?"

"Harry?" Hawthorne asked.

"In the bunker he asked me to call him Harry. So, how we going to hang Harrison?"

"If he's smart, he left the state, so it's on you guys," Stanski said, nodding at Hawthorne.

"He's smart, all right," Hawthorne said.

"Alaska," Davecki said.

"Most likely," Stanski said.

"No doubt about it," Hawthorne said. "I'm heading up there tomorrow."

Davecki marveled at the fact that there had been no mention of the watch yet, or the jars tossed into the snowbanks. Better than a real bank, he thought. The crime scene inventory would not include the snowbank gold.

"Carczak had a house in McCarthy," Hawthorne said.

"McCarthy? Isn't that where he died," Davecki said.

"Allegedly died," Hawthorne said.

"You mean he's still alive?" Stanski asked.

"Well, his body was never found."

"You seriously think he could be alive yet?" Davecki asked.

"Declared dead, but never any remains," she said.

CHAPTER 24

Davecki studied Stanski.

Stanski didn't return the gaze. He busied himself mopping up the last bit of homemade maple syrup with the waffle that Davecki had just served the deputy.

"You're lucky to still have a foot, buster."

"Good thing my powers of recovery are legendary."

Stanski clanked his fork down on the table, lifted the plate, licked the last smears of syrup, butter and waffle shards.

"You're disgusting."

Stanski's muffled voice slithered from behind the green fluted Depression glass plate, "Thanks." He plunked the plate down, continued, "Man that syrup is too good to waste." He licked his lips. "Well…" he pushed back from the table… "gotta go meet up with Warden Dan."

Davecki limped to the sink carrying plates.

Stanski said. "The Crick Dicks found Harrison's camp out south of Winneboujou. Thanks for breakfast."

"Careful out in that Winneboujou country," Davecki warned.

"Oh yeah. The Trickster." Stanski said. "I'm guessing Dan has seen all the tricks Winney has to offer. Besides, Harrison wasn't there. Dan knows the terrain."

"Yeah. But that ol' Winneboujou, he can mess things up fast."

Stanski smirked at Davecki. "Like your theory that Winneboujou started the pandemic as a bet with that other guy?"

Davecki sighed. "Seagull and his big mouth. It's Nanabozho for your information."

"You still believe that malarkey?"

"Ever see that movie, *The Gods Must Be Crazy?*"

Stanski moved toward the door. "I saw it but can't remember anything about it. Why do you ask, white man?"

"How about *Under the Dome* by Stephen King?"

Hand on doorknob, Stanski asked, "What rabbit trail is this going down, Alice?"

Standing at the sink, Davecki answered, "Your cynicism is impressive, Diogenes."

"Who?"

"Never mind. Just be careful out there in Winneboujou land."

"I'm not a believer."

"Believer or not, powerful people, great legends, forces beyond our understanding are always at work. Never hurts to be careful."

"You should have kept that in mind out on the Rez."

Davecki said nothing.

"Later, gator," Stanski said. He exited without fanning the door this time.

While doing dishes, Davecki pondered. I wonder what really happened to Carczak up in Alaska? For that matter, what happened to Kitty Love up there? From where and why is all this evil emerging? He put his palms down on the bottom of the empty sink still full of hot sudsy water. I bet Harrison killed Carczak. After all, he slept with the guy's wife. Umm, that warm water feels good. But why kill the goose that laid the golden egg? I need more heat. Carczak must have been a piece of work. Be a good time for sauna. You'd think Harrison would be smart enough to keep Carczak alive until finding the gold. Davecki pulled the plug. Tourists do die up there. Bears, cliffs, Sasquatch on vacation from Minong, the occasional back-to-the-lander driven mad by black flies and mosquitoes or, if really unlucky, the snows of March and April.

Davecki let the hot sudsy water lower itself around his wrists and hands and fingers. Not fun starting sauna in this cold weather. Gotta dress Daniel. Worse than having a puppy. Maybe a nap first. A good nap always helps.

Davecki's dream went from lounging on a cruise ship deck next to a woman in an itsy bitsy yellow polka dot bikini to swimming beside Brekken Hawthorne in a tropically warm underground pool of turquoise water to, "Snap out of it, asshole." He realized it was no dream when Harry Harrison jammed the nasty 9mm muzzle into his nose.

"Huh? Okay. Okay," Davecki said, shifting his weight up higher in the recliner and wincing as his old pal Daniel complained. "You're supposed to be in Alaska," he said, automatically reaching down to rub his left leg.

"No, you don't," Harrison said, whacking the right side of Davecki's head with the pistol barrel.

"Ouch! Man! What's your problem, Harrison?

"You reaching for an ankle gun or something."

I thought this guy was supposed to be smart, Davecki thought. "Right. I got a drop gun tucked into my pajama holster."

"You're a real smart-ass, you know that?" Harrison stepped back, keeping the nine leveled on Davecki.

"So I've been told. What's the drill now?"

"I want that watch. I was being generous until you screwed up my chance at the gold."

"You weren't planning on killing me?"

"Why would I do a stupid thing like that? All I wanted was the gold. Your paranoia ruined everything. Now the only thing of value left is the watch."

"You could have fooled me with all the lead you were throwing in my direction."

"I was just trying to get you to stop."

"Right. Your daughter said it's fake."

"She's entitled to her opinion. I know different."

Davecki considered saying that he turned it in as evidence. Never good to lie. "It's in the drawer in the nightstand in the back bedroom."

"Don't move," Harrison waved the pistol at Davecki as he backed away toward the rear of the trailer.

"Really? I was thinking I'd jump up and Chuck Norris you from behind with my swollen left foot," Davecki said.

"Right. You managed to get away on it once already. You're a tough old S.O.B. I'll give you that, so don't get fancy." Harrison vanished down the hallway.

I wonder if he's going to shoot me this time? I should put up a struggle. Why? Why not just accept it. You've had a good life. It's been real and it's been fun, but this isn't real fun. He closed his eyes and prayed, Our Father who art in heaven....

"You're awfully calm," Harrison's voice interrupted Davecki's version of Last Rites.

"What's a mother to do?" He lifted Daniel Day-Lewis, pulled up the pant leg exposing his black foot. "They gave me OxyContin. A very calming effect it has, it has."

"You take the cake, pal. Where's your cell phone?"

Is that a glimmer of light at the end of the tunnel, Davecki wondered. "Believe it or not, it's in the fridge."

Harrison's blue eyes widened. "Seriously?"

"Yeah, the battery's shot and I read on the Internet that putting it in the fridge will make it last longer."

"You're really weird, you know that?"

"So I've been told."

"I gotta admit, For a weirdo, you're kinda appealing. Plus, you're lucky I had a good night and a nice breakfast. Don't get out of that chair for an hour. If you do and if I bump into you again I might not be in such a good mood."

"Umm, one more thing," Davecki Columbo-ed. "How do you manage to vanish and reappear like Casper the not-so-friendly-ghost?"

"Don't push it, copper."

"Ex-copper. I'm retired, you know."

"You don't act like it. Now sit tight in that chair for an hour. Got it?"

"You da boss," he said, picking the remote up off the end table. "Mind if I watch *Family Feud?*"

"I love that show," Harrison said. "Knock yourself out."

Davecki remoted the TV, listened to the refrigerator door open and tried to guess what 100 men answered when asked what they would say when held at gunpoint.

CHAPTER 25

Daniel Day-Lewis' pain had been as far away as Alaska and was now returning for a visit. While Steve Harvey practiced his knack for making money, Davecki looked at the bottle of Oxy on the side table. Umm, that's what I'll serve Daniel for din-din, Davecki thought. Struggling with the cap, he wondered, did I just get robbed? It could have been a dream, I suppose. He shook the bottle. The rattle revealed that one pill remained to rule them all. Was Harrison really still in Wisconsin? How am I going to get another prescription? From the comfort of his recliner his peripheral vision noticed movement in the circular driveway. Is that a dog team going past? Heroic cousin Longmire would figure this out, Davecki thought. The cap resisted his efforts while reality resisted his efforts at perception.

What was that line from ET? This is reality, Steve? Or was that Steve Harvey who said that. Maybe one hundred women could answer that in a survey.

Finally.

The cap cooperated and beloved Oxy sent Daniel off on another adventure, likely to Alaska in pursuit of either a criminal mastermind or a comely FBI agent.

Didn't matter.

Didn't matter.

Didn't matter.

"Dave! Dave!" Stanski's voice intruded in either a dream or reality.

"What!? What!?" Davecki answered.

"You left the fridge door open. What's with you, man?"

"Huh? Huh?" Davecki muttered.

Stanski glanced at Hawthorne who knelt beside the recliner. She picked up the empty pill bottle. Wiggled it at Stanski.

"Oh oh," Stanski said.

"World of hurt," Hawthorne said.

Davecki opened his eyes slowly, looked at Hawthorne, his face slowly reorganizing itself into signs of cognition far behind. Distant synapse closed. He said, "I love you, Brekken. I thought you were in Alaska."

"I love you too, Dave. Got back this morning. How's the foot?"

"What foot?"

"The one the doctors almost amputated, fool," Stanski said.

"Ease up," Hawthorne said. She stood and touched Stanski's arm.

"I just love how hospitals these days toss people out so fast," Stanski said.

"That's better," Hawthorne said, de-touching his arm.

"It's all about cash flow," Stanski said.

"You're Mr. Compassion, Stan," Hawthorne said.

"Yeah, Stan. That's better. You're such a good friend. Did you close the fridge door, buddy? You're the Labrador I never had buddy, ol' buddy, ol' pal o' mine."

"Yes. Why'd you leave it open?"

Hawthorne shook her head at Stanski. She sat down on the

end table, patted Davecki's arm and repeated Stanski's query with a hundred times more sympathy. "Do you remember leaving the fridge door open?"

"If it was the gas stove, you'd be dead, Dave."

"I die daily, man. So what's the big deal?"

Hawthorne glanced at Stanski, eyes steely.

Stanski shrugged.

"Harrison must have left it open."

"WHAT!?" both cops asked.

Cool, Davecki thought. Their alarm sobered him a little more. "Yeah," he said, taking a big breath and raising his arm, "He took my watch." As he moved, so moved his left foot. "Owie, owie," he said.

Settling his foot and resorting to what tiny shred of reason he possessed, Davecki said, "Maybe it was a dream. Maybe it was the drugs. Maybe it was real, but, if you found the fridge door open, it's entirely likely Tom, Dick and Harry Harrison isn't in Alaska but is still roaming around the north woods stealing watches, and evading your best efforts at catching him and his dog team."

"But the team went back to Love and Remington," Stanski said.

Davecki laughed. He stared at Hawthorne, "You ever been swimming in Belize?"

"Huh?" Hawthorne asked.

"Never mind." Davecki looked at Stanski. "Stan, if there are dog and sled tracks on the driveway, then it wasn't a dream."

Davecki looked from Hawthorne's beautiful face to Stanski's tired-looking mug, wondered if he was being too hard on the new dynamic duo. I always thought they'd make a good pair, he thought. Then he thought, Hawthorne and Stanski doesn't sound as cool as Stanski and Davecki.

"Harrison was here?" Stanski asked.

"Need I repeat myself, fool?"

"Okay. Good. You got me back. Good for you," Stanski said with a smile.

"The drug is wearing off," Hawthorne said, grinning.

Stanski shook his head, said, "Try to talk some sense into him. I'm going out to the driveway to see if there's dog poop and runner tracks."

She laughed her crystal laugh, green eyes dancing. "We've got to get you off these," she said, showing Davecki the orange empty stairway-to-heaven bottle.

"I'm confused," Davecki said.

"It'll get better, little buddy," she said. She patted Davecki's arm again, asked, "If Harrison was here, it had to be for one thing. You still have the watch? Or did you pawn it already?"

Davecki gulped. "The FBI knows?"

She grinned. "The FBI knows all, sees all, tells as little as possible."

"Well, I didn't pawn it. If I was dreaming about Harrison, it should be in the nightstand drawer in the back bedroom. If it's gone, Harrison let me live for some odd reason."

"His profile isn't pathologic. Unlikely to kill for sport or pleasure. More of a profit kind of crazy."

"Could've fooled me when he was shooting at me out on the Rez."

She stopped at the passageway, put those lovely fingers on the doorframe, "Yeah, well, he was desperate at the time. But, from what we've put together, he's more greedy than homicidal."

"Him and the rest of the world," Davecki said.

"You got that right," she said and exited stage left.

"He was here all right," Stanski said, red right returning.

"No watch. Open drawer," Hawthorne chimed in from port.

"Penchant for leaving things open," Davecki said. "Add that to your psych profile. At least he didn't burn down my shack in the woods. Anything in the profile about a fascination with fire?"

"Not that I recall," Hawthorne said.

"You're not one of those gifted profilers, are you?" he looked at Hawthorne.

Stanski said, "Careful around her, Dave. She can read people like an open book, buddy."

"Tell me about it. Well, the fact that Harrison is still in this neck of the woods narrows the field of fire considerably," Davecki said.

"Yeah," Stanski said, "But what I can't figure out is how good he is at evading detection."

"And with only a team of dogs to boot," Hawthorne said.

"Easy peasy," Davecki said.

"Oh yeah?" Stanski said.

"Do tell," Hawthorne said.

"Not until you give me a squeezy," Davecki grinned. He winced as he levered the recliner down and struggled to his one good foot.

"Spill, Dave," Stanski demanded.

Stretching out his arms, Davecki, grinning said, "Not until we have a group hug."

"Hugging is out now," Stanski said. "The Oxy making you forget a little thing like a global pandemic?"

"You're no fun," Davecki said.

"So, how is he pulling off his disappearing act?" Hawthorne asked.

"It came to me in a dream. They're the infamous ghost team of the Muskeg Swamp."

"What?" Hawthorne said.

Stanski said, "You're such a jerk, Dave."

Davecki, tottering on his good foot, trying to save Daniel any discomfort, laughed and said, "The Ghost Team of the Muskeg Swamp travels the dimensions teaching brotherhood and making all worlds a better place."

"The drugs are making him goofy," Hawthorne said.

"Goofy is normal for him," Stanski said heading for the kitchen. "I need coffee."

"Normal is just a setting on the dryer, pal," Davecki grumped.

Hawthorne, green eyes wide to let all the strengthening sunlight and BS in, followed, saying, "Good idea, Stan. A strong dose of caffeine might put things right. That redeye from Anchorage to Minneapolis takes forever."

Davecki followed, limping along in his automobile print PJs. "I know what dosage would put things right, but I doubt I can get another prescription."

"That's the last thing you need, nimrod," Stanski hollered from the lead dog position.

"Caffeine will have to do," Hawthorne said from swing.

"Bummer," wheel dog Davecki said.

"This coffee is good, Stan. Thanks, man," Davecki said.

"Yeah. Not bad for a man," Hawthorne said.

The men looked at her.

"You guys are so easy," she grinned.

"Pfft," Stanski pffted. "So, how's Harrison getting away so easy, Mr. Peasy?" He looked at Davecki across the table.

Straight faced, Davecki said. "You're not much of a detective, are you Stan? How about you, Brekken? Your highly trained FBI brain figured it out yet?"

"Hardly. Do tell, oh great detective," she said.

"Ex-detective. Retired," Davecki savored another sip. He drew the moment out.

"I'm going to have to kill you, Dave."

Grinning, Davecki said. "I'll give you a hint."

"Oh, please," Hawthorne said.

"Don't," Stanski said, "begging only makes him worse."

"Settle down children, Columbo is about to speak." He sipped.

The children remained mute.

"Where's Harrison's camp?"

The children looked at each other. "You got to be kidding me," Stanski said, his usually happy face scrunched into irritation.

"What? What?" Hawthorne asked.

"You're a real pain in the arse, you know that," Stanski said, standing. "We gotta get going, Brekken."

"Okay. I give," Hawthorne said, standing.

Stanski shook his head, moved toward the door. "I'm not going to give him the satisfaction."

"Would someone please talk sense?" Hawthorne asked.

Davecki laughed. "He's got Winneboujou on his crew!"

"Jerk," Hawthorne said.

"Now you're getting into the swing of things, Agent Hawthorne," Davecki said.

She followed Stanski, leaving the door open.

CHAPTER 26

Chuckling as he hobbled to close the door, Davecki put some actual thought into how, in reality, in this day and age…how could Harrison evade all the technology with just a team of dogs? "Try, try, try, to understand…he's a magic man," song lyrics by Heart popped into his head. Right beside the wonderment about Harrison, the brain felt the pain of his throbbing foot and cried out for more OxyContin.

He limped to the dining room table. I should fry some potatoes and eggs. Or I could go to Duluth and score some Oxy. Or I could go talk Doc Ami into another prescription. Or…you know…. The only way Harrison could pull his vanishing act is…is with help. What did Harrison say? Something about having a good night and a good breakfast putting him in a good mood?

I'm lucky to be alive, I guess. For now, anyway. He returned to his chair, eschewing fixing food. He rubbed his blackened foot. Tears fell from his eyes. "Poor Daniel. Poor, poor, Daniel," he muttered.

Wonder if Double Malt Gault is still dealing, Davecki wondered.

Stanski and Hawthorne have something good going, passed through his mind.

I'll have to stand up to cook breakfast. Poor foot. Poor foot-foot.

Por-favor foot. Please foot, get better. Fastly, please.

Rising up, rubbing his wet cheeks, he launched from the table, wobbling to the cupboard. Standing there, both hands on the opened doors, the memory of Harrison discovering the cupboard full of gold returned. The depressing reality of Grape Nuts by comparison stared back. Be nice if even one quart of gold was there beside the cereal, he thought. Maybe in the spring.

Who cares? He told himself as he poured neither grapes nor nuts. Not my problem. I'm not a cop anymore. Grab a spoon from the drying rack. Wobble back to table.

Damn Stanski. Keeps coming over asking for help and then stealing my girl to boot.

Dang! Forgot the milk. Wobble to the fridge. Wobble back with moo juice in hand. We bulls wobble but we don't fall down, he thought of the joke as he plunked the milk jug down.

"HA!" he haahed.

Hawthorne's nobody's girl, let alone Stanski's.

Why did they give me only five pills? What's wrong with people? Don't they know what it's like to have a foot get mangled and frozen? They don't know what it's like to be Rolex-less in Wisconsin? Why is the last word in Wisconsin, sin?

"BANG!" Davecki pounded the table with his balled-up fist.

His left thumb caught the end of the spoon in the bowl as he pounded. The spoon did a back flip. The spoonful of not sugar didn't make the medicine go down. Splashing across the table and floor, the tiny brown nuggets pittered and pattered all over the table and floor. "Damn it!" he cursed, grabbing the spoon and throwing it in the direction of the kitchen sink. "God!" he cried, picking up the bowl and flinging it towards the sink, cereal flying in all directions.

"Arrgh!" Davecki yelled. Standing, he knocked the chair backwards and humped across the nutty floor. Now both feet hurt, he thought as the crunch, crunch, crunch of cereal sounded below. He picked up the bowl that had missed the sink by a Tommy John margin and landed on the counter next to the microwave. Tossing the bowl into the sink, repeating same with spoon, he flipped the faucet lever up. Tears came. Water flowing from two wells. He turned and looked at the cereal covering the dining room table.

If Hawthorne was sitting there, I wouldn't be so Grape Nuts, he thought. I'd talk. She'd listen. That would be nice. "Okay. Okay," he said out loud. "Settle down, Alphonse." He shut the water off, turned and leaned back into the counter.

"Our Father who art in heaven, a little help here?" He looked at the empty chair. What would I say if she was sitting there? If Jesus was sitting there, what would I say? What would Jesus do?

Heal my foot. Maybe. Or just listen? Maybe there's a Bible verse. "Okay. Okay," he went to the fridge. Inside, half a carton of eggs, a chunk of cheddar and a bottle of catsup. No wonder Harrison left the door open. Slamming the door, Davecki limped back to the table. Sitting, he swept the scattered Grape Nuts to the floor, shoved the milk jug aside and rested his aching head on the table. The cool tabletop felt good on the skin of his forehead. Lifting his head up, he bonked the tabletop trying to drive some of the coolness into his hot brain. That felt good too. "Bonk," he hit the table harder with his head. "Bonk-bonk." The bonking felt good enough to continue. With each smack-down, teardrops splashed to the dusty tabletop.

"Geez, Dave, you having some sort of spell or something?" Seagull asked.

Looking up, there stood the giant logger, truck driver, fisherman, sneaker-upper-on-cray-cray-person. Seagull looked at

Davecki with a mixture of worry, humor, and confusion swirling across his face and eyes.

"I can come back to cut the wood later if you want to finish whatever you're doing."

"No. No. I'm okay. I'm just going grape nuts with the pain and all the OxyContin is gone."

"Shit, man," Seagull said, still standing in the doorway. "You should never have got on that shit. It makes the pain worse in the end."

"How would you know? Shut the damn door!"

"No need to be rude, Dave," Seagull said. He stepped in, closed the door. He pulled out a chair and tested its load-bearing capacity. "They handed me a golden ticket perscription when I had my gallbladder out. Took a week to get over the operation. A year to get over the Oxy."

"Really?" Davecki looked at Seagull. "Shouldn't it be prescription?"

"Whatever," Seagull said.

He's no Brekken Hawthorne, that's for sure, Davecki thought. Or Jesus, or the Father in heaven. But, he's what God sent. He'll have to do.

Before Davecki could start professing his woes, Seagull said, "I had to get Danny to pee in the bottle for me so I could pass the DOT whiz-quiz. Drove the semi loaded, and not with pulp. Got in a fight with Double Malt Gault when he cut me off. Even a month in rehab didn't help much."

He's talking way more than Jesus would, Davecki thought as he rubbed his left leg under the table. Then he encouraged even more talk, asking, "What'd you do to get clean?"

"Who says I'm clean, man?"

Davecki's eyes widened... "Really? Sweet!"

"HA! Just shittin' ya man. Just trying to show how messed up you are." Seagull leaned forward in his chair. It squeaked and creaked under the strain of his great weight. "I saw Stanski and his new squeeze at the end of the town road. He told me about your foot, man. And Uncle Seagull is here to make living better but not with chemistry. Now get up off your sorry ass, cut the pity party, and get dressed man. We got wood to cut."

"I can't cut wood with this foot."

"No shit? Seriously?"

"Seriously."

Seagull stood, the trailer shuddered. "Can you run a picaroon? Can you limp around, pick and drag chunks away? How about mixing gas or fetching me a glass of water? Can you do that, you lazy, crazy, old fool?"

"Get out of my house, Seagull."

"Gladly, but you better be on deck outside in ten or I'll come back in and beat your sorry ass into submission. Got it?"

"Jerk."

"If you say so. Now shake a leg, Alphonsy."

Davecki peered at the looming Seagull. I believe he would cause me great bodily harm, he thought.

Like the old arthritic black lab with hip dysplasia, Big Dog, Davecki struggled to his one good foot, "Come on, Daniel," he said, shooting Seagull a look of death. "Mr. Sasquatch here doesn't understand."

"Who's Daniel?"

"My left foot," Davecki said, chuckling. He limped toward the back of the trailer, laughing at his own joke. "MY LEFT FOOT!" he called out, laughing louder as he crunched across the Grape Nuts floor. "MY LEFT FOOT!" he bellered even louder just because it felt good.

Seagull watched Davecki. Shook his hairy head. "You're a weirdo, you know," he called out.

"So I've been told."

"Ten minutes, pal," Seagull said, turning to the cold hard job of cutting up twelve cords of oak in winter in Wisconsin.

"JERK!" Davecki yelled again from the hallway.

By the time he got back to the bedroom, he was crying again. It's crying time again, you're going to leave me, he Dean Martin-ed. Big tears rolled down his cheeks. Pain shot up his left leg as he unzipped the Carhartt bibs and struggled the left pants leg past the white gauze dressing. More crying and sobbing as he sat on the edge of the bed. Guiding the neoprene foot gadget Essentia provided for Daniel…more tears. "Sissy!" Davecki mewed. Putting a sock on the good foot, he looked at the open empty-of-Rolex nightstand drawer. Wasn't ever really mine in the first place was it, he pondered.

"JERKS!" he yelled. He leaned over and rammed the drawer closed with a loud bang.

I'm going to freeze my foot all over again, helping that big galoot. Why am I letting him boss me around? I'm paying him to cut wood. I should be the boss, Davecki thought as he hobbled down the hallway.

Davecki saw through the porch window that Seagull was sitting in his Chevy pickup and not out cutting on the pile of wood.

Grabbing crutches and stepping into the cold and onto the wooden steps someone had shoveled, Davecki was about to yell at Seagull, asking what he was doing, when the Chevy power window sank into the doorway like magic. Seagull hollered, "Get your sorry butt in the truck, buster. Got to get some good nutrition in you buddy. We're going for breakfast."

He's a magic man, Davecki sang inside his pain-addled brain.

CHAPTER 27

As usual, Queenie's eggs and hash browns made everything better. On the way back, the men were silent as the radio made noise through the truck speakers. Davecki wondered how the log truck driver/fishing fanatic could afford the Vexilars, the new phone, the nice truck, child support, alimony, and eating out for breakfast. Probably has a gig going with Gault, he thought.

Seagull reached out and touched the radio face, shutting down the blather. He turned into Davecki's driveway and parked beside Timber's big pile of hundred-inch oak. The pile looked mountainous with all the snow heaped upon it. The top of the snow pile was a good four feet taller than the truck roof. Seagull sighed and said, "No time like the present." He popped his door.

Not your typical drug addict, Davecki thought. Drug dealer maybe, but a meth head? Not.

Davecki fumbled with the aluminum crutches. "Crutches on ice in December," he muttered, as he skittered his way to the back of the truck where Seagull stood at the tailgate of the Silverado.

Might as well be pistols at dawn in the town square, he thought.

"You need a walker, man," Seagull said, wielding his chainsaw file, sharpening the teeth on the Husqvarna. Saw looks new too, Davecki observed. Something's fishy, he thought. Maybe he's selling fish. As Seagull filed the chisel teeth on the chain, Davecki wondered why he was afraid to ask directly. "Seems like you're doing okay, with Hayward not taking wood," he said.

Seagull didn't look up from his meticulous sharpening. He grunted a bit, answered, "You're sure as hell nosey."

"I'm a retired detective. I'm hardwired to ask questions."

The round file scraped across the tooth in question. A crow cawed down by the river. Scrape, scrape, scrape. File, file, file.

Seagull grunted again, said, "It was rough at first. Then along came Covid and PPP money. Lotta paperwork, but easy money and lots of it. I don't care if I ever go back to work. Plus, if you must know, they give you a new phone if you switch plans. Plus there's no interest and I haven't paid the bill for two months. They can cut me off any time they please. As for the saw, credit card. The truck'll get repo-ed soon no doubt. Satisfied?"

"Yup."

"You going to get a walker?" Seagull asked.

"Nope." Mentally he admitted, a walker would be better, dang it. But never with green tennis balls on the leg ends. Well, maybe one green and one yellow.

"Suit yourself," Seagull said, tossing the file into the battered green toolbox next to the two gallon mixed-gas can and beat-up looking gallon plastic bottle of bar oil. He jerked the saw up, walking toward the woodpile. As he walked he jerked on the starter rope with the practiced rhythm and coordination of someone who'd started a chainsaw thousands of times. It was the backwoods ballroom dance where the partner could cut your leg off at one misstep.

I wonder what ever happened to Partner chainsaws, Davecki wondered as he reached into the pickup box, retrieving a red-handled picaroon. He tottered after Seagull. The saw started and Big Hairy Man kicked snow away from log number one of 399 to go in the twelve-cord pile. I love the smell of chainsaw exhaust in the morning, Davecki thought. Thank you, Robert Duvall and whoever wrote that great line. Stanley Rubrik? No, he invented that cube thing. Francis Ford Acapella? Maybe. Or was he a songwriter? I could sure use some Oxy he thought, watching Seagull dice the hundred-inch wood into five twenties.

He's a magic man, Davecki thought, watching Seagull play the Husky like a Stradivarius. Or is it Stadivarious? Could be various strads, he thought. Then he thought, I wonder who is helping Magic Man Harrison. He's partnered up before. Him and Carczak were a team. Dog teams just don't outrun snowmobiles, squad cars, and radio waves.

A scowl on his big round face, Seagull lifted the orange chainsaw and pointed toward the severed blocks of wood with the nose of the bar.

Better clear those chunks. Davecki let the crutches fall where they may. He swung the picaroon on wobbly legs and, as picaroons are sometimes wont to do, the point glanced off the frozen wood, veered around faster than a hunting hound treeing a bear cub. The point ended up hooking Seagull in the calf.

"Arrgh!" Seagull yelled. He killed the saw and tossed it aside with a clang and clatter. Grabbing the red pick handle out of Davecki's hands he pulled the point from his leg.

"Sorry. Sorry," Davecki said.

Seagull just grunted, grimaced and pulled the picaroon from his leg.

Davecki backed away. The big man limped to the truck's tailgate. As Seagull retreated, Davecki observed the tidy rectangular hole in Seagull's Carhartt bib pant leg where the pick had penetrated.

Seagull threw the pick into the pickup box. It knocked the tool box over. Files, plugs, chainsaw wrenches, tip greasers and raker gauges flew in all directions.

"Sorry, Seagull," Davecki said.

"I shoulda known better." Seagull shook his big shaggy head as he hopped toward the passenger door. His gray beard swished like a mop forth and back. He opened the door and hopped backwards into the passenger seat, opened the glove box, and like a magic man, produced a slender orange bottle with a white child-proof cap. "Here you go, loser," Seagull said, tipping the bottle toward Davecki.

"What's that?"

"Oxy, you dumbass."

"Seriously?" Davecki held out his palm.

Seagull tipped a pill out. "Seriously. Gault can be intimidated."

They looked at each other as Seagull tipped out his own pill.

Sweet, sweet relief.

"Even a blind dog finds a bone now and then," Seagull said. His stupid grin reminded Davecki of a happy sled dog puppy.

Soon he had no foot. Daniel Day-Lewis was in his happy place again somewhere far, far away. The cold December air seemed more Hawaiian than Wisconsin. Davecki looked at the crutches fallen like the pick-a-stick game from a million years ago. The skewed aluminum crutches looked a million miles away. Seagull had started the Silverado. Davecki had gone to the tailgate, pushed aside strewn tools and wondered why people hated winter so much. This ain't so bad, he thought, looking around at the piles of snow Rhoweder had pushed up. Shoulda looked at the temperature. Shoulda copped me a quart of gold. Shoulda pawned that watch. Shoulda asked Hawthorne out the day I first met her on the river. Who is helping Harrison?

Davecki studied the box of Seagull's pickup.

No sign of dog poop or husky hair.

Man, this OxyContin stuff is fantastic.

The throaty exhaust rumble of a car approaching made some sort of sense to Davecki, but not a lot. He sat on the tailgate swinging legs forth and back like he was sitting on a playground swing in August.

The car rumble turned into a Dodge Squad. Behind the windshield, Stanski and Hawthorne. The triangulated trio studied each other for moments bordering on discomfort. Stanski popped his door, got out, walked around the front fender to Davecki, said, "You know it's ten below, don't you?"

"Seriously? I thought this was Tahiti, Stan. See the palm trees?"

Stanski studied Davecki a few moments. "Are you wasted?" He looked back at Hawthorne. Summoned her with a nod. Her door popped. Stanski studied Davecki again. He looked over his pal's shoulder through the rear window to Seagull's bulk in the Silverado passenger seat, passenger door wide open.

"Unbelievable," Stanski said.

"What's up?" Hawthorne asked.

"Hi-ya beautiful," Davecki said. "How about you give me a big smooch?"

"What?" She looked at Stanski, her pretty face scrunched up.

"Oxy," Stanski said.

"Unbelievable," Hawthorne said.

Stanski went around to Seagull. Muted and muttered conversation filtered back to Davecki and Hawthorne.

Davecki stared at Hawthorne, worship on his face. "You're the most beautiful creature God ever created." He waved his hand toward heaven. Hawthorne had to dodge the gesture. "You and Stan make a great couple."

Hawthorne grinned. "You're out of your mind, Alphonse."

The pickup door slammed behind them. "Get in the squad, Dave," Stanski said red right returning. "Back seat, man," he added as he walked around the end of the truck. "You drive the squad, Brekken. I'm driving Seagull's pickup."

"Where we going ol' buddy ol' pal o' mine?" Davecki said as Stanski grabbed Davecki by the elbow.

Hawthorne, grabbing Davecki's free elbow, looked across Davecki to the deputy, eyebrows raised. "Yes, officer. Where we going?"

"Detox."

CHAPTER 28

"Why are we helping him?" Kaylee asked.

Grim-faced Kitty Love's knuckles were white atop the steering wheel. "It's complicated."

A dog truck is a remarkable vehicle. There are stacks of feeding dishes, plastic buckets, ropes, axes for chopping frozen doggy dinners, clumps of harness hanging, empty and full Redpaw bags, and of course, that one Redpaw bag repurposed as the poop bag, usually with a shovel handle sticking out. Organized chaos for the most part. And the smell, don't forget the smell, a combination of blood, sweat, and tears, along with the hint of emu oil and other medications.

Combine a dog truck and a veterinary van and the chaos ramps up a notch, especially when there are no dog boxes and the pack is free to flop down anywhere in the back where there's floor space or a corner to curl up in.

"I don't care how complicated it is. I want to know," Kaylee said as the van slowed to a stop at the top of a small hill on a desolate town road deep in the bowels of Lowland Township.

Love put the van in park. A dog in the back offered a muted bark. "We're fine. Fine," Love spoke to the rear, looking in the rearview mirror, checking on the dogs. She let out a long sigh, "I suppose you deserve to know." She glanced at Kaylee in the passenger seat, looked out the windshield at the frozen landscape. She reached out and turned the heater fan to low. The decibel level retreated from dangerous to tolerable.

Another long Love sigh.

Remington twisted around in her seat. "Just tell me."

Love stared down the road. She gripped the steering wheel again. "Harry Harrison is your grandfather."

"What?!!"

"You heard me."

Remington stared at Love who stared down the road as the fan hummed as the world turned.

"I…? I…?" Kaylee stuttered.

A dog in the back whined. Another dog growled.

"I know," Love said. "Very complicated." Her jaw muscles flexed as she looked in the rearview mirror, adding, "Settle down back there."

"You mean…?"

"Yes," Love said, "Total SOB that he is, Harry's my father so I have to help him. Sorta. Maybe. It's a bitch."

"Oh, my God," Remington said.

"Adoption was the best thing I ever did for you." Love said. She opened her door, paused her exit, looked at Remington. Her tired face wore a tortured expression. "Just stay calm and don't say anything to piss him off."

Fifty feet in front of the vet van, a dog team emerged from the woods and strung out along the town road.

"Right now we need to get the team in and get Harry to his shack down south. He's on the run again."

Love slid out of the van, slammed the door. Kaylee Remington followed Love's moves, though her face wore the mask of shock and awe.

It was cold out, but who cared? This was winter in Wisconsin. What else could it be? The air was made the more frigid by the silence of the team and the handlers as Love and Harrison unhitched dogs in silence. Kaylee stood at the back of the van, mute as she took each dog handed off to her and stuffing them past the half-open door to keep the pack from escaping.

When they got the sled inside, Remington looked at Harrison's grizzled face, stared into his deep set eyes, said, "Grandpa?"

"WHAT?!! What did you call me?"

Kitty Love came around the corner with a handful of gang line. "What's going on here?"

"YOU TOLD HER?" Harrison's gloved hand lashed out.

Love ducked.

Kaylee didn't and the blow struck her square in the face, knocking her down.

"You SOB!" Love yelled. She swung the gang line at Harrison, who deflected the assault with his left arm and smacked Love in the chest with his right.

"Arrgh!" Love yelled, dropping the line. "I've had enough of you!" she hollered. She ripped the zipper of her parka down, reached into an inside pocket and pulled out a knife.

"You and Jack and your knives. Give me that!" Harrison said. He lunged at Love.

Love was quick. She unsheathed the blade as she stepped away from Harrison's lunge and swung the blade at him.

Scrambling to her feet, "Mom! Grandpa! STOP!" Kaylee yelled.

Harrison's disarmament plan turned into disaster as the deflected knife arched into Kaylee's parka.

"Uhh," was all Remington managed.

"Oh, my God!" Love screeched.

Harrison rebounded and turned on Love.

"YOU!" Love yelled. She swung the knife again.

This time it found a home in Harrison's midsection.

"You bitch!" Harrison clutched at his belly.

"MOM!" Kaylee cried.

"Get in the van. Both of you," Love commanded.

Harrison, his face white behind the black whiskers, said, "No! No ER!" He opened his parka. A deep black stain of blood spread across the Carhartt bib over his belly.

"Oh, my God," Kaylee said.

"I've had worse," Harrison said. "Take me to the clinic and stitch me up, bitch," he said, glaring at Love.

"Let's look at you, Kaylee," Love said.

Remington unzipped her parka. A slash on her sweatshirt showed a halo of red around its perimeter. "I'm okay. It hurts, but I don't think it's deep."

As Love bent toward Remington's wound, Harrison grabbed her knife hand and knocked the bloody blade to the snow. He picked it up, brandished it at the two women and said, "Get me to the clinic…now!"

As the van hurtled down the back roads, man moans and dog whines came from the back of the van.

"I think he's hurt bad," Kaylee said, looking into the back where Harrison sprawled amongst the dogs. "I smell blood," she added.

"He'll be fine," Love said. "He got shot three times in a bar fight and survived. It's you I'm worried about."

"I'm fine. He looks bad."

"Don't worry about it. He's tough. He got stabbed twice in prison and lived."

Kaylee turned in her seat, looked at the driver. "Why haven't you told me any of this before?"

Love glanced at Kaylee, "You didn't need to know." She turned the van onto the highway, said, "I shouldn't have said anything."

"I deserved to know."

"Deserve is overrated by a long ways," Love said.

"Arrgh," from the back.

Kaylee turned toward the rear. "He's hurt bad."

"I'll patch him up." Love said.

At the clinic Love opened the rear door of the van. Dogs leaped out, scrambling and clawing. "Come on, Harry. Let's get you sewed together again."

More dogs jumped down from the van.

"Harry?"

Standing next to Love, Kaylee said, "Grandpa?"

"Shit," Love said as she climbed into the back. She scuttled across the floor, leaned down to Harrison's face. "Shit. Shit!" she said.

"What?" Kaylee asked as dogs frolicked in the background.

"You son of a bitch," Love said, staring down at Harrison's dead eyes. "You never once did me an ounce of good in your life and now you're doing it again."

"What's going on?" Kaylee asked.

"The SOB bled out. He's dead."

"NO!"

"Yes," Love said, frisking the corpse. "I'll take this," she said, sticking Harrison's pistol inside her parka. She crawled out of the van, looked around. The dogs were having fun chasing each other, barking, yipping, and biting. "Shit-shit," Love said. "They'll put me away for life now." She looked at the building, the garage, the inside of the van, and eventually at Kaylee.

"What are we going to do?"

Love put her hand on Kaylee's shoulder. "Sorry to say this to you, child. But it's no longer we. I've had enough of this and I'm not going to prison."

"Mom?"

"I abandoned you once before and you made out all right. Better for not being in this family," she said as she got on the snowmobile parked next to the garage.

"You can't leave me. What am I going to do?"

Love's hand went to the key, "Go back to your Alaska family. You'll be way better off with them. I suggest you go visit that goofball detective and tell him you want your watch. It's a Rolex and it's worth a couple of million at least."

Love looked long at Remington. She shook her head. Started the snowmobile. Looked one more time at Remington, made a poor attempt at a smile, and fled.

CHAPTER 29

Nobody takes a drunk seriously. If they do, they seriously need a program. Davecki chattered like a chickadee in the backseat of the squad. "Brekken. Brekken. Bo Brekken. Banana nana bana… bo Brekken. You take the cake. A great couple you and Stanski make. Hard, hard, hard to rhyme Brekken. Gonna take a little time, gotta think things over…" he sing-songed.

The cold December day was gray with low clouds. The monochrome of winter spread across the frozen fields and woods outside the cage Davecki occupied. "Brekken, Brekken, peckin', banana-nana-bo-Brekken…Brekken," he repeated.

Heavy sigh from the front seat.

Settle down, Alphonse. "Gotta read between the lines. Can't stop now. Change my lonely life….Gotta love Foreigner." Get it together, the more sober part of Davecki's brain tried again.

"What's foreign, David?"

"I want to know what love is. I want you to show me," Davecki sang.

"Oh yeah," Hawthorne said, "Foreigner."

Davecki grinned. He looked outside. Oh man, am I going to have to apologize after this wears off. "Nowhere left to hide. There's been heartache and pain but OxyContin has finally found me," he warbled. "How you doin' Daniel?" Davecki asked. He looked down at his foot. Poor, poor foot, he thought.

"Who's Daniel?" Hawthorne asked.

"My left foot," Davecki replied. He looked up and out and through the windshield. A red and black Dodge dually van that was probably an ambulance at one time in its life whizzed past in the opposite direction. The remains of Davecki's brain that wasn't opioid liquefied saw the bold lettering across the side in less than a second. VETERINARIAN.

"You know Stanski loves you like a brother," Hawthorne said.

"That's a good thing? But, yeah. I know. He loves you and me and all the flowers and the bees."

Heavy sigh.

"Birds fall down from the trees around you, Brek."

Heavy sigh.

From the drug-hyped maze of neurons deep in Davecki's brain, *follow that van,* drifted up like January ice fog from the Brule River.

"Vantastic," he muttered.

Heavy sigh from up front.

He considered how best to convey sobriety and seriousness. He lowered his voice. "Brekken," was all he said.

The well-trained FBI professional in the front seat called upon her discipline to ignore Drunk Dave.

Okay, get it together, Alphonse.

"Seriously, Brekken...."

Beautiful green eyes flashed to the rearview mirror.

"Agent Hawthorne...."

More green eyes. Baby's got green eyes in the rearview.

"Okay. Okay. I'm sobering up a little, Agent Hawthorne. I

know you're not supposed to listen to drunks or believe drug addicts spouting from backseat cages, but I'm about to tell you something very important. I hardly know what it is, but all I know is I'm supposed to tell you."

Hawthorne let a few moments of consideration pass as she flicked eyes from the road ahead to the road less traveled in the rearview mirror.

Davecki put his head in his hands and scrubbed his temples. "Oh man, this is so weird," he muttered.

"What's weird, Dave?"

"Being so wasted. So drunk. It's like being a teenager all over again."

Heavy sigh. More driving.

Again from the deep, like the depths of Lake Superior deep, *time's a-wasting*.

"We gotta follow that van," Davecki said.

Something in his voice had changed and Hawthorne noticed. "What? What van? What are you talking about?"

"I can't know, Agent Hawthorne. But somewhere, somehow, some way, it makes sense that we turn around and follow that van."

"What van? Where?"

"The one that we just met a few miles back."

"We met a van?"

"It was like an ambulance." Davecki grabbed his head again, manipulated it forth and back, twisting it around like it was a basketball in Maggy Gandolfson's magical hands. His neck bones crunched, being stretched to their constricted limits. If he could have done a Beetlejuice with his head, he would have.

"I can't stop following Stan," Hawthorne said.

"It's important, Agent Hawthorne."

"Stop calling me that."

"I'm trying to get your attention."

"You're drunk. Wasted."

"I'm sobering up. I can't tell you the why or where-for, but that veterinary van we met…."

In a flash everything made sense. Two words made the crazy mixed-up world of gold, greed, good dogs, and a fish, and a watch, transmogrify into instant understanding.

Kitty Love.

"Oh, man, Agent. I got it. I got it. We gotta go after them."

"Who?" Hawthorne asked.

"Time's-a-wasting, Brekken. Call Stanski and tell him I got it figured. He'll know. He'll tell you I'm an idiot-savant and encourage you to turn this train around."

Heavy sigh.

Hawthorne fished her phone out, said, "Hey Siri."

"Siri, Siri, Siri, po-piri, banana-bana po-piri," Davecki sang as Hawthorne talked on the phone.

"Okay. Okay. If you say so," Hawthorne said.

"What'd he say?" Davecki asked, his fingers interwoven in the cage wires between driver and detainee.

"Hard to believe, but he said I should listen to you." She applied the brakes and made like Ward Bond to turn the wagon train around.

"Aww-right, aww-right, aww-right," Davecki said. "Me and Matthew McConaughey all the way."

CHAPTER 30

Hawthorne's phone rang.

"Roger, that," Hawthorne said into the cell.

The back-seat babbler sang, "Rodger, Dodger, Dooger, Deeger. They're Santa's reindeer in an alternate universe," Davecki said. Adding, "What did ol' buddy ol' pal o' mine Stan have to say about the sit-z-ation?"

"He said trust but verify when it comes to listening to your nonsense. That he'd take Seagull to the E.R. for a tetanus shot and a look at the puncture wound and get him into detox and rehab and catch up with us."

"That'll take him a week," Davecki said. "Two things suggest themselves in this delicate situation."

"Okay. I'll bite. What two things?"

"Beats me. You're the federal agent. You said the FBI knows all." Davecki laughed.

Heavy sigh in the front seat.

Chuckle in the back. "You're so easy," Davecki said.

"So. Where we going?" Green questioning eyes in the rear-view mirror.

"We're off to see the Kitty, the Wonderful Kitty of Oz."

CHAPTER 31

"Won't we need a warrant or probable cause?" Hawthorne asked.

"Warrants? We don't need no stinking warrants," Davecki answered. "We're after the treasure of the Sierra Madras, don't 'cha know."

"It's Madre. Not Madras. You're still wasted. I should be driving."

"We're just paying Love a friendly visit."

"In a squad car?"

"There is that," Davecki said. "I'll tell her my truck broke down and you're driving me around. That I'm bringing my new pet to the vet."

"You still drunk? That's ridiculous," Hawthorne said. "Besides, you'd need a pet for that?"

Davecki looked at Hawthorne. Face deadpan. Evil grin lurking just out of sight.

It took the sharp mind of the FBI agent three seconds to figure it out. "YOU! I ought to kill you right now and put myself out of your misery."

"Sweet," Davecki returned his gaze to the road less traveled ahead of them. "You sound just like Stanski now. You two are going to have a great marriage. Can I be your Maid of Honor?"

"You're drunk."

"Ma used to say, 'when the booze goes in the truth comes out.' Stan, he's the marrying type."

Hawthorne stared at the road ahead, her face radiating concern.

"The long and winding road to your door…."

"Would you please stop that?" she pleaded.

"What? What?"

"Your stupid singing. It's irritating."

Davecki looked ready to burst into a song-answer. Hawthorne cut him off asking, "We'll need probable cause to stop the van if we catch it."

"Probable cause? What's that?"

"You know…a reason to detain someone?"

"Oh, you mean like, 'I stopped you because you have a tail-light out? Or I thought I saw you weaving.'"

"But you're not a cop anymore."

"That's where you come in."

"This is messed up. We need a reason to stop someone."

"Oh, yeah. Right. Like…. Umm, how about…'you crossed the fog line. Are you okay?' Or, 'It looked like you didn't have your seatbelt on.' Or, 'I was bored and I saw your long blonde hair and you looked young and pretty and I'm single and'…."

"I get it, Dave." Hawthorne studied Davecki who studied the road to perhaps perdition ahead. He kept his eyes forward knowing full well she was lasering him. Finally she said, "This is messed up."

"True," Davecki said, still staring down highway not-61 un-re-visited. "But, I'm not going to get my watch back if we play by the rules."

"I could lose my job."

"Never thought of that," he said, looking at her, seeing the concern on her face. "How about we go home. I'll get my truck. I'll go it alone and if I get into trouble, I'll call you guys."

"What do you mean, if?"

"Well, there is that." He started humming.

"At least you're not singing," she said. "How is your foot?"

"Daniel? He's fine. Whining as usual, but you just get used to these drama queens. Always demanding attention. It's best to ignore them."

"If you say so," Hawthorne said, turning into Davecki's driveway.

Coming around the slight bend that hid the trailer from the road, two sets of astonished eyes beheld the vet van parked square in the middle of Davecki's driveway.

"Well, I'll be. The mountain has come to Muhammad again."

"How convenient."

"Welcome to Davecki's world," he said, grinning like the Cheshire Cat.

"So messed up," Hawthorne said, her own Cheshire grin overtaking her beautiful face.

"But oh so fun."

"You can say that again..." Hawthorne said, raising her hand to stop Captain Obvious from speaking.

Davecki attempted to speak....

"No! Don't you dare," she said, adding, "What now?"

"Let 'er develop, me father used to say. Just go with the flow, me mother used to say."

She parked behind the vet van. Davecki popped his door open, "I'm thinking maybe it's best for the moment if you stay put. Let me see who Horton is. Okay?"

"Fine by me."

Davecki limped wide around the back of the van. "Hello?" he called out.

A yip and a whine of the canine kind echoed from within the box.

"Anybody?" Davecki called, walking closer to the driver's door. As he got to the vet van's window, Kaylee Remington's shock of blonde hair, all smooshed against the window, appeared. Davecki peered around to see Remington's pale face, open mouth, closed eyes.

"Hawthorne!" he yelled. He pulled the driver's door open. Remington slipped sideways. Davecki caught the falling musher and fell back himself. Barks and yips erupted from the back of the rig. He staggered backwards, landing on the tall snowbank. Together they slid down to the frozen snow-covered driveway. He scooted out from under his burden and put his cheek to Remington's petite face.

"Status?" Hawthorne said as she rushed to Davecki's side.

"Breathing but unresponsive."

"Keen grasp," Hawthorne said.

"Obviously," Davecki answered, feeling for a pulse.

Hawthorne unzipped Remington's parka. The formerly small stain of dark blood was now spread out wide and black around the slash in her Redpaw sweatshirt. "Stab wound," she announced.

"Keen grasp," Davecki said.

Hawthorne pulled out her phone.

"What are you doing?" Davecki asked.

"Calling 911."

"No time. They'll take weeks to get here. Or at least half an hour," he said. "Get her in Stan's squad."

They scooped up the dainty dog lady and eased her into the back seat where her blood could add to the unique chemistry.

"You driving?"

"Gotta quick check the dogs."

"She's bleeding, Dave."

She'd want the dogs to be okay."

"Okay. Make it fast."

Davecki opened the vet van's back door. Barks and doggie stares. Rampart and all the other "R" dogs flashed their icy eyes. Like a tsunami of fur, ten dogs scrambled out. Davecki's pathetic efforts to stop them were, in a word, pathetic.

Hawthorne leapt out of the squad. "Now what?"

"Get her to the E.R. Fast. I'll try to contain these rascals and figure out what's going on."

Hawthorne dodged dog bodies back to the Dodge Squad and backed down the driveway at speed.

Listening to the roar of the car exiting stage left, Davecki had no idea who the actual dogs were and what "R" names went with what animal. He called out, "Raptor?"

That's not it. Not one dog paid a bit of attention. Romping continued unabated.

He tried all the "R" names that came to mind, "Rebel! Randy! Rivka! Rosie! Roberta! COME!"

Ten canines just wanting to have fun Cindy Laupered all around the yard and driveway, leaping, barking, growling, biting at one another. Snow flew in geysers as powerful haunches launched loads of doggie fun this way and that. Barks and yips echoed off the frozen trees.

So carefree, Davecki thought. He planted butt on the van's back bumper. Watched the doggie free-for-all. He noticed that Daniel Day-Lewis wasn't complaining as much. Nice, he thought, watching the carefree dogs cavort.

Heavy sigh. Wonder if I'll ever be as carefree and goofy as them.

Then, like two cold hands reaching into his warm collar and encircling his hot neck, a creepy, crawly feeling interrupted his ponderment. The middle of his lower back got chills. The cold folds in the skin slithered upwards, chilling flesh as it went. The spectral hands and scary chills made his bladder lose a little control. His hair stood on end.

He turned and looked into the back of the van. Wedged

between half a dozen bags of Redpaw dog food, and the dog sled, the prostrate form and pale dead face of Tom-Dick-Harry Harrison looked at him with glassy, sightless eyes.

"Lord, help me," Davecki said. He shook his shoulders, cracked his clavicles and climbed into the van. Grabbing a wrist and feeling for a pulse he already knew didn't exist, he found no sign of life and a two million-dollar Rolex.

Sweet, Davecki thought as he unclasped the band, retrieved his golden ticket and pocketed it. He stepped outside and dialed 911.

Waiting for cops to come.

Is there anything that slows life down more? Sitting on the back bumper of the vet van turned meat wagon, Davecki took out the watch. He put it on his wrist and liked the weight of it there. I can't keep this and be rich at the same time he thought. If I sell it I'll have the money but not the feel of it. Plus if I sell it I told Seagull he could have half. Too bad, so sad Seagull. He's got plenty of money even if he acts like he doesn't.

A dog ran past, yipping and yupping as another dog chased it into the oncoming evening.

Let 'em run. They're free for now. Gotta feel good to them. He wiggled his wrist again. Sure feels good, he thought. I'm keeping it. But then I'd have to share with Seagull and Stanski. That would be hard. He took the watch off. Twirled it in his fingers.

A dog ran up, panting. The dog's blue eyes searched Davecki's face for some sign of affection. Davecki, fixated on the watch, ignored the love in front of him. The wise dog didn't take no for an answer, it stuck its slick black nose and warm furry snout right into Davecki's hands.

"Hey! You! Quit bothering me."

The dog pushed harder, twisted its head, rubbing its ears against Davecki's unresponsiveness.

"Okay. Okay, you little brat. I wonder what your name is?" he said, setting the watch aside. "I bet it starts with an R." He grabbed the cozy dog behind the ears and head, scratching and twisting.

R Dog fought back with delicious resistance, intensifying the pleasure of a good old fashioned petting-wrestling match.

"Who's a good dog?" Davecki asked.

The answer never came because two other dogs tore past, barking and yipping. R Dog couldn't resist. It pulled away and sprang off in pursuit.

So much for love and affection, he thought. He picked up the watch, twirled it once, thought, not today, Dave, and returned it to its rightful, or wrongful, place on the dead man's wrist.

CHAPTER 32

Officialdom is a mess, Davecki thought as his driveway became more and more clogged with vehicles of every ilk. The Coroner had a new County car. The M.E. had a new County car. Used to be a time when one intrepid individual was the M.E., Coroner, and the marriage and dog license guy who showed up driving his station wagon, usually with a kid or two staring out at the body because they were at basketball practice when the beeper went off. Beeper? Who even remembers those now? As yet another deputy showed up in yet another new squad, he wondered, how many cops does a dead criminal require? The FBI arrived driving an 80-thousand-dollar Suburban. Hawthorne must have called. How many cell phone bills does the FBI get every month? The sheriff showed. Big Jeb Dinkle from the Tribal Police showed. Two wardens on brand new Skandics buzzed up off the snowmobile trail. Is that a stealth Cobra helicopter hovering above?

This is messed up, Davecki thought, watching the wheels of justice grind slowly and exceedingly fine. The three-ring circus of ten dogs romping went unnoticed. The partridge in the maple tree behind the garage fluffed its feathers against the cold wind picking up from the north.

While everyone is standing around officializing, whoever killed Harrison and stabbed Remington is getting a lot of escape time, he thought.

A dog stalked up, kicking snow with its rear paws, scratching snow up like mini-explosions under his paws. Was it Raptor? Or was it Reggie? Maybe Raymond. Davecki reached down to pet the pooch. "Who's a good boy?" he said, scratching the dog's neck. The dog blinked its eyes. The left eye was deep brown. The right, bright blue.

"Now which one are you? Reaper? Randy? Roper?" The panting dog decided that fun-run time was over and fun-massage time was the order of business. It jumped up, placing both paws on Davecki's chest. "If you were my dog I'd name you Grim," he said, rubbing the dog's back while dodging the flashing pink tongue trying to lick his face. "Grim Reaper." Yep. A perfect name for this situation he thought, while glancing at the partridge in the pear tree that was actually a grouse in a maple, but, who's keeping track of that, he thought. On the dog's collar, a name tag. Rampart. Oh yeah, Lead Dog, Davecki remembered.

Lead Dog under control due to ear scratching and neck rubbing, Davecki watched the rest of the pack. Their cavorting was significantly diminished. Looks like the ten lords a-leaping grow weary, he thought. What a miracle dogs are. I wonder if there's a strong string of canine chromosomes in my DNA somewhere. I should probably try to get them rounded up. If one or two of them decide to take off and go cavorting in the woods they'll be tasty wolf snacks by morning.

One nice thing about being a semi-civilian in the middle of full-blown officialdom…nobody of note pursuing their professional duties notices the civilian off to the side roughing up a dog's head and shoulders. "Better get you tied up, Grim,"

Davecki said. He hooked gloved fingers into the husky's collar and together they went unnoticed to his garage. With his free hand he poked the code into the opener. The overhead door rolled up. Entering, he grabbed the coiled-up clothesline from summer and fashioned a bowline through Grim's D-ring. He took an errant clothespin off the rope and tossed it on the cluttered workbench and took a half-hitch around the bench leg to keep Grim Reaper at bay.

The dog, being doggish, fleetingly looked at the departing Davecki with a crystal clear ice-blue eye, then looked around his new kennel. Only one thing was required to make his new home a home. The dog lifted leg, baptized bench leg, walked to the end of his tie, and flopped over on a dusty rug for a nap.

Two dogs were kicking up a minor snow squall as they circled a maple tree chasing a gray squirrel just out of leaping range up the trunk. The squirrel clung motionless to the tree bark as the dogs barked up at their tormentor. Wish I had some treats, Davecki thought as his cell phone chirped.

Looking at the Unknown Caller on the screen, for some reason known only to his guardian angel, Davecki decided to answer, thinking that, under these unusual circumstances, the call might *not* be a robot figuring out a way to sell him a funeral package. "This is Dave."

"Hawthorne here," the voice said in his ear. "Remington's going to make it. She said that Love stabbed her."

"So Kitty is the culprit," Davecki said.

"What happened?"

"Harrison and Love argued. Turned violent. Kaylee intervened. She was stabbed. Accidentally, so she says."

So it was Kitty who kept the knives sharp, Davecki thought. "What were they fighting about?"

"Gold and Iditarod dogs," Hawthorne answered.

Gold and good dogs, Davecki thought. "Why did Kaylee drive to my place?"

"Hard as this is to believe," Hawthorne answered, "she thought you could be trusted. Obviously she's a terrible judge of character."

"Keen grasp. How'd she find my place?" Davecki asked.

"Ever hear of a thing called Google Maps, troglodyte?"

"Very funny. Any clue as to the whereabouts of one Kitty-less-than-lovely?"

"No. But Kaylee thinks she'd head back to Alaska, a non-extradition state, by the way."

"But this is a federal issue now. Better to flee to South Carolina or Missouri," Davecki said.

"The only states that haven't adopted Uniform Extradition," Hawthorne said.

"Either way, she's still got to be in Wisconsin yet."

"Stan put out an APB and a BOLO on her."

As he paced and talked and took in all the news that was fit to print, one of the pack dogs decided to pay attention to the wanderer. The dog stood at full alert, nose extended toward Davecki's outstretched fingers. The two enacted the northern Wisconsin version of the Sistine Chapel.

"Stan wants a word."

"Yo, Dave. You remember what brand of snowmobile it was at Love's place? Need to add that to the BOLO and APB."

"A Polaris."

"Thanks. Cop flurry over yet?"

"No. But it's winding down. I'm still trying to assemble a pack of dogs that is running amok."

"Good luck with that. Seagull is refusing detox. He says he's going to sue your insurance company and you shouldn't take it personal."

"That's great news," Davecki said, "now I don't have to share the Rolex money."

"Don't forget me," Stanski said.

"Who is this again?" Davecki asked.

The curious dog sniffing Davecki's fingers relaxed enough to get a scratch behind the ears and two fingers under its collar.

"I gotta go," Davecki said. "Just caught me dog number two."

"What's your plan, man?" Stanski asked.

"I think it is finally time for me to visit Harrison's camp out south. Love might go there looking for the watch or more gold."

"Seriously?" Stanski asked. "What about the Trickster Winneboujou?"

"You know I don't believe in that hooey, Stan."

"Make up your mind, will you please? Your flip-flopping is confusing."

CHAPTER 33

By the time officialdom evaporated to their separate lairs, Davecki had all the dogs tied up. The van was still in the driveway waiting to be towed. He dragged the sled from the back and commenced to figuring out how to turn a dog pack into a team.

Hooking dogs to a sled isn't rocket science.

But it is a lot of fiddle. And a bunch of faddle. A lot of fiddle when learning on the fly. Throw in a faddle or four when it's cold and getting colder. Everything is stiff…rope and mainline and harness. Zippers stick. Velcro gets iced. Sled runners stick. When very cold, even clothing creaks and cracks in frosty complaint. Fingers however, are marvelous little creatures. Davecki discovered that fiddling with harness and hooking up rammy, looking-for-adventure-and-whatever-comes-their-way, dogs is not a job for gloved hands.

What a miracle the body is. Instead of stiffening up and working "worsely", active naked fingers, supplied with hot blood from a thumping heart, get a shoutout from the cerebrum.

Cerebrum brags to the hypothalamus at how fine the fingers are. The hypothalamus takes the cerebrum's pride in stride and urges Old Heart to pump even more blood to busy little digits.

Good Old Heart, always there for a musher wanna-be.

Dog brains, however, are not impressed with low functioning Hooman who knows not, "what he are doing". Doggos get impatient. They jump and jerk against the tugs snapping the mainline against the sled. The barking is loud, cacophonous even. This one or that will hop the mainline, getting tangled while Silly Hooman figures things out.

One thing Silly Hooman will never accomplish is calming down the calamity of a dog team in waiting. The team is raring to go. Fug-git-about-it-Hooman-let's-get-going!

Then a most remarkable event occurs. The moment Hooman yells, "Go!" the pack mayhem of howling, barking, leaping, crazy-to-go-dogs turns into a silent team digging in forty clawed paws using powerful strokes of their mighty haunches to do what they were born to do.

Run! Pull! Go!

In an instant the wild bunch transmogrifies from chaos to order, an order that inspires a most satisfying serenity that Hooman can thoroughly enjoy, provided he does the simple thing required.

HANG ON.

Then comes sweet solitude.

Settled in on the runners, watching the team surge and sway in the soft evening light, the snaps and buckles flashing softly in the headlamp beam, the unique peace and pace of mushing dogs rewards silly Hooman with wealth more than gold. The soft silent swish of runners on snow. The creak of the sled. The rustle of the bag. The tingle of cold air pushing past nose and face and ears. "Me all face," Eskimos say with deep understanding.

And there's the descending darkness, the drooping eye of a suddenly sleepy winter's day. The sky thickens and the stars wink back into existence even though they've been there all along. The stark dark trees roll past like an old-time black and white movie. And there's the mind movement induced by the magic of mushing.

I could've starred in *Iron Will,* Davecki thought. Not. I wonder where my watch is right now, he thought. He lifted his left arm. It felt light without the Rolex in its rightful or wrongful place. Not my watch anymore.

Illuminated by the light of the headlamp found amongst the detritus of the mushing gear, the ten undulating dog backs looked like a single organism. Man, these musher headlamps are powerful, Davecki thought as the snow shushed below his one old and one new boot. Dogs are powerful too, he thought, recalling how the team brought Harrison to the bunker in the blizzard. No wonder Iditarod dogs are so expensive. Where are we going, my little ones?

It's like a dream, Davecki realized. I'm a tiny bubble of light, a corpuscle of life flowing along the dark trail connected to all the trails in Wisconsin and the world. I'm a Zen Master, mushing, being pulled by fabled creatures of old. Dogs as old as time. Mythic animals with spiritual wisdom and animal power beyond my comprehension. Dogs, good dogs, Davecki marveled, are unfathomable.

The corpuscle of light and life in the darkness came to a bridge. The team stopped of their own, or maybe Rampart's accord.

Now what? Davecki wondered. For all his ability, Rampart can't tell me what's next. Probably turn them around and head back. Enough of this fun, he thought.

He stood on the runners contemplating the near future. The wheel dogs looked back into the light. In fact, the entire team was looking back to see what he was looking forward to see. What Davecki saw was ten bushy tails a-waving, ten tongues a-lolling, twenty eyes a-sparkling. He turned the headlamp toward the treetops. Not a single partridge in a popple tree.

Recognizing the frailty of Hooman, Rampart in lead walked

back toward the lump of indecision failing in his role of mastering and commanding.

As the team reversed itself, a crow cawed in the dark mid-distance.

The crow's wake-up call pulled Davecki from the magic of mushing to the awareness that Daniel Day-Lewis was unhappy. I should be home in my recliner elevating my wound. Shoulding on yourself, Davie. Bad sign, he thought as the dogs got all jumbled while self-reversing. Now that they're tangled they're not going to take off without me like they did with Remington. When was that? Last year? Or yesterday?

Davecki quit thinking and commenced to commencing the true act of mushing, separating dogs who were tangled and trying to understand what is required of them. Not to do justice and love mercy, but to get straightened out and head back home. He strong-armed the pack this way and that, got them sort of lined out, and managed a sled pivot to make the run back to the trailer.

Then what, he wondered as the team suddenly leaped into action and took off running back down the trail the way they'd come.

Only one thing wrong with pran, Charlie Chan.

Silly Hooman stood and watched.

Now I know how Kaylee Remington felt, Davecki thought as the sled winked out of existence like a star vanishing at dawn.

Only this was what, seven o-clock in the evening or so? He wiggled his Rolex-less wrist. Man, I miss my Rolex, he thought. If I ever get that thing back, I'm keeping it. He rustled into the inside pocket of his Carhartt, pulled out his phone. 7:30 and no signal. Nothing to it but to do it. He and Daniel began the long limp home.

CHAPTER 34

The problem with OxyContin, other than being unable to rhyme it well, is…Daniel Day-Lewis eventually has to deal with reality. Davecki's limping home soon devolved into sitting on the snowbank of the day watching the night roll away.

OxyContin. OxyContin. OxyContin, Daniel Day-Lewis sang. The chorus got louder each time Davecki limped again.

Where oh where are you tonight, Davecki chorused back. I searched the world over, looking for OxyContin, you met another and poof you were gone.

I'd settle for ibuprofen, Lewis grouched. Never settle for second best, Davie boy. Vitamin I is a poor cousin to richy-rich Oxy. Or d-lala.

You took a fine time to leave me Ox-ee, Davecki thought. He thought about Seagull. Where oh where are you tonight, Gull? Chasing after Gault?

Sweating from pain, he limped to the snowbank made by a trail groomer, backed into a slouch on the snow, relieving a little of Dan's suffering.

What an idiot, he thought.

You fool. You fool, he thought.

He rubbed the pain tears away with the back of his mittened hand, sighed, almost sobbed, looked up and, through the naked branches, saw one huge reason life in northern Wisconsin in the winter is worth living.

The heavens above were glorious. Deep black dotted with millions of stars that devoted their entire existence to shining down on a tiny human in dire straights or straits.

"Man," Davecki muttered, "that is something else."

You're talking to yourself again, old man.

The silence was complete. The only sound, his heartbeat pulsing in his ears. The lub-dup faded as Daniel Day-Lewis calmed down. Gazing heavenward he thought, I can see why Aristotle figured the heavens were rotating spheres. They're alive with some sort of flowing pulsing ether.

If I can't have Oxy I'd settle for ether, Lewis called from far, far away.

Ether of us would, Davecki rebutted and returned to the hypnotic winter night sky above.

It could have been a minute or an hour. Sorta like being in the hospital, 20 hours without knowledge of time passing. The sound of a speeding snowmobile approaching disturbed his hypnosis.

Before he had a chance to sit up and wave the machine down, the blinding headlight blew past going at least a hundred miles an hour. Or fifty. Either way, that's how people get killed, he thought. The red taillight turned the billowing snowflake-wake of the speeder into a huge orange blossom. The machine vanished down the trail. They shouldn't make those things so fast, he thought. Then the whine of the machine's powerful engine changed pitch in the pitch-black distance.

Coming back? Davecki wondered.

Then silence.

The whining sound grew louder.

Yep, Davecki smiled. Saved again, he thought. Thank you, Lord, he prayed.

This time the headlight approached like a sane person was driving. It came to a stop adjacent to his snowbank throne.

Kitty Love got off the machine.

Can I take that thank you back, Lord?

"I'm going to regret this," Love said, pulling the 1911 from inside that ever present parka.

Not as much as me. Or maybe it should be I, Davecki thought.

"Gimme the watch, loser."

CHAPTER 35

Davecki made motion to de-watch his arm, but instead, reached up and clicked on the headlamp, flashing it in Love's eyes.

"Aww!" she yelled, raising her gun hand to protect her vision.

Davecki dove forward, knocking Love down. The gun went flying. His momentum carried him to the Polaris seat. Despite the pain in his foot, Davecki swung Daniel over the seat and took off.

Leaving Love behind is the best thing I've done to date, Davecki thought.

One thing wrong with pran, Charlie Chan.

Love always finds a way.

She scrambled around in the snow, found the pistol and sent hot lead in the direction of her fleeing affection.

First Harrison, now Love, Davecki thought. Guess Pat Benatar was right, love *is* a battlefield.

One thing about that menace to society, high-capacity magazines…throw sufficient lead in the direction of the target…success happens.

"Owie! Owie! Owie!" Davecki yelled when the law of averages got him in the back. He twisted away from the pain. The sled hit the right snowbank. Then it hit the left snowbank. Then it said, enough, ceased from its bumper pool, and slowed.

No, you don't, Davecki corrected. He squeezed the throttle. Weak from being shot, his easy-squeezy on the throttle was none too powerful. The sled kept fleeing Love, but none too fast. You know, he thought, they should make these things faster. Faster than a speeding bullet would be nice.

But no.

Instead of the Everly Brothers and *Bye Bye Love*, the Polaris, no matter how tightly Davecki squeezed the throttle, Polaris went slower and slower. Suddenly Davecki had a vision of looking down on the scene.

There he was, brown-Carhartted back hunched over a crawling-slower-than-a-porcupine-in-deep-snow Polaris snowmobile in the darkness of night in the wilderness of northern Wisconsin. The witch-finger trees waved up at him as he hovered high.

Hello, trees.

So, this is the view my guardian angel gets to see all the time. Pretty sweet, he thought. So cool. Angels have it made. Flying around looking the world over from up here and then slipping into human form to help people unawares, then zipping up to heaven to check the records kept in those big thick heavenly books where all the sins and compassions are recorded. But then, those big old books have likely been replaced by terabytes and pixels. Another fine pixel you've gotten yourself into, Dave.

"Get a grip, Alphonse," Davecki heard.

What? Where? Who? He wondered.

Then…back in his body.

Davecki thought, this snowmobile reminds me of Jim Carrey on that trike in *Dumb and Dumber*. Come on, baby! Move! Get me to my safe place!

I don't wanna, Polaris said instead. It came to a dead, pardon the pun, stop.

Then…back in the balcony looking down.

Davecki watched a dark figure on a white trail advance on a Polaris stalled in the middle of the winding pathway through the trees.

Uh oh, Davecki thought.

The Carhartted figure on the sled slipped off the bloody seat to the left and flopped out on the trail like a car-hit coyote.

Man, my left side is getting the tar knocked out of it lately, Davecki thought. He watched Kitty Love ooze toward Davecki's certain doom. Wait a minute, he thought. That's my certain doom down there.

What's going on?

Part of his brain heard the Polaris idling in his right ear. Part of his brain, or limbic system, or spirit, or soul, or whatever, could feel-sense-know Love's footsteps as she closed the distance on the object of her desire. Or maybe it was object of hatred, he thought. They're twins, he realized.

The voice that had just told him to get a grip said, "Will you look at that."

"What? Who?" Davecki said.

"Look down the trail," the voice said.

Back down the trail a ways, a ten dog team of dogs approached. This time with a musher.

"Love is coming to get you, Dave," Get a Grip Voice said.

"Really?" he answered out loud.

Did I actually hear that? Is God actually talking now? About time.

"Shake a leg, Dave," Get a Grip Voice urged.

Okay. Okay. Geez. Lighten up. I just got shot in the back. Show a little compassion will you?

"There'll be time enough for compassion when the shooting's

done, Dave. Right now, time to head 'em up and move 'em out. Unless, of course, you want to come with me to the light."

Why does God sound like Christina Aguilera, he wondered.

Then he was crawling for all he was worth back onto the patient, idling Polaris.

He flopped across the seat like a long scarf hung over the back of a chair, noticing as he did, the blood thereupon. Slippy, he thought in Canadian.

Draped over the slippy seat like a limp dishrag, gripping the throttle handle was tricky, but he managed to get a grip…thank you disembodied voice from on high—Alphonse squeezed the throttle with all his strength.

The sled coughed a minor protest and shuddered forward, steady by jerks.

"Owie! Owie! Owie!" Davecki yelped. Why does everything have to hurt so bad?

"Life is a bitter veil of tears and pain, mon frère. Now, will you give 'er a little more gas, please?" Get a Grip pleaded.

Quit bugging me, whoever you are, he complained.

"I'm going to ignore that request. Shake a leg, partner."

"Nag, nag, nag," Davecki muttered as he squeezed the throttle a bit more.

Polaris, used to running fast and free at full throttle, wasn't getting the hang of this new turtle pace. It chugged and coughed again, cleared its throat, and shuddered forward like a horse being led to water but not drinking.

Speaking of lead. From behind about twenty yards, Kitty Love, yelled, "Stop, or I'll shoot!"

Seriously? Shouldn't it be, "Stop, so I have a fixed target?" If it didn't hurt so much, I'd laugh, he thought, and he laughed. You know, he thought as the pain seared his body, some OxyContin would be nice right about now and he squeezed the throttle with what he considered Herculean strength.

Polaris responded to the gentle throttle caress with a little more speed.

Again, from the balcony, Dave saw Love assume the position. She widened her stance, raised weapon, locked both elbows, gripped 1911 firmly in right hand, clasped left hand 'round right.

"BANG!"

Lucky dog. Lucky dog. While he had no additional strength to squeeze the throttle more, he did have sufficient energy to notice the dashboard exploding and the windshield shattering from the impact of the 9mm bullet. That would have gone right through my heart if I had been sitting up like the guy on the snowmobile sign, he thought. Then he thought, forgot to count. Wonder how many rounds she has left?

"You're going to have to decide," Get a Grip said. "Either go toward the light with me, or, if not, you should probably concern yourself with getting more distance, buddy."

Stanski? That you, buddy?

Davecki tried to sit up and squeeze more go-go out of the new love of his life, Polaris.

But Polaris knew Supremely that *You Can't Hurry Love* especially after absorbing multiple gunshot wounds.

Then again with the hover-vision.

From above Davecki watched as Love gained on him, or on that hunk of bleeding carcass that used to be him down there, now that he was up here, or was he down there?

CHAPTER 36

One thing about dogs, they know way more than Silly Hoomans realize. Lead Dog Rampart, seeing Kitty Love assume the firing position, did what had to be done. He leapt to the rescue like Rin Tin Tin.

Silly Hoomans on and in the sled to the rear didn't have time to bark a command.

Rampart had the plan. Silly Hooman, the one with poking needles and sharp knives, needed trampling.

Silly Hooman on the sled needed some real love.

Rampart ran over Love and ran to Davecki, commencing to lick face.

The rest of the team compressed like an accordion finishing a Chmielewski polka all around Love.

"Get off me, you mangy creeps!" So fickle Love is.

Team dogs like to obey. Especially around a veterinarian, lest the needles come out. Rivka and Raymond and the rest pulled forward dragging the sled right on top of the struggling veterinarian.

The whole team gathered around Shot Hooman and commenced to licking, nose-poking, pawing, and giving those tiny little love nips with their shiny front teeth.

Hovering above, watching the team ignore all known Covid protocols, Davecki heard again, "How you doing?"

Without diverting his attention from the drama below, he answered, "Not bad. Not bad at all." He patted his chest and belly. "In fact, I'm feeling fantastic. Like I'm on Oxy only better."

Finally he looked away from the doggy love fest and felony arrest below. On his right there was a very nice-looking woman. Or maybe an ultra-handsome man. For sure a person. A glowing individual of Davecki's height. A very bright oval face. Sparkling eyes and a serene smile, wide and welcoming. Pretty teeth, if teeth can be pretty.

"Who are you?"

"Some call me Get a Grip Voice, but I'm better known as Kelly." A slender hand that literally glowed against the darkness below raised like a magic wand. "Nice to finally meet you, Alphonse."

"Kelly? As in boy Kelly or girl Kelly?" Davecki asked, shaking hands.

"Neither," Kelly answered. "And both." The smile grew to face busting proportions.

"Oh man," Davecki said. "You're an angel, aren't you?"

"Not just any angel."

"You're my guardian angel?"

"None other."

"Wow. I'm honored."

"Feeling's mutual," Kelly said.

"No kidding? Hey, do you know Clarence Odbody?"

"Clarence Odbody is a fictional character, Alphonse."

Davecki frowned. "Seriously? Too bad."

"Now…Henry Travers? Nice guy. You'll like him if you stay, Alphonse."

"Would you mind calling me Dave? Alphonse is what Ma always called me when I got in trouble."

"I know. And you always managed to get into plenty of trouble. Although that was a nice move, putting the watch back. Of course I'll call you Dave. I am yours to command." Her tender, slender, dusky blonde eyebrows lifted like a teacher waiting for a student to grasp the concept.

When it dawned on Davecki, he asked, "Can I see your wings?"

"I would if I could. Sorry, wings are old school."

"Oh man. That's terrible news. I always wanted to see angel wings," Davecki said.

"Oh, there's lots of retired troglodytes that still have them. You'll see. But for modern angelizing, wings are too slow. New technology now. We use handheld transporters."

"Like Star Wars?"

Kelly frowned. "It's Star Trek, Dave. You're not that good with fiction, are you?" Her impish grin enhanced the bright twinkle in her eyes.

"Yeah. Not my strong suit."

Kelly raised her left wrist, showed a device banded there.

"Looks like my Rolex," Davecki said.

"About that," Kelly said.

"I know. I know," Davecki cut in. "I returned it."

"Yes. Of course. But it was a struggle wasn't it... Alphonse," Kelly said, grinning.

"You're giving me attitude? I thought guardian angels were supposed to always be nice."

"After what you've put me through, *Dave,* I'm entitled to copping a little attitude."

"Man, you're kinda uppity. You know that Kelly? You got a supervisor or anything?"

"Umm, yeah, but I don't think you'd like him. He's kind of a stickler for things like little white lies."

"Sheesh, lighten up, Kelly. I'm a detective. Little white lies are part of the job."

"Retired detective, as you're so fond of pointing out, so you have no excuse. Especially for lying to yourself. Right, Alphonse?"

A little staring contest ensued until Kelly smiled like a winner, looked aside and said, "Now. About the business below. What are you thinking?"

Davecki looked down. The unfolding scene moved like molasses in January. Only it was still December. "Geez. I don't know. This feels great," he said, patting his chest and tummy again.

"Yup, no more aches and pains in heaven," Kelly said.

"You look a little familiar."

"You'll get used to that if you decide to stay. Everyone knows everyone from everywhere," Kelly Angel said. "So, what you thinking? Stay here or go back?"

Looking down, the slo-mo sped up. The dog sled conveying Deputy Dog and FBI Goddess came to rest smack dab on top of Kitty Cat Love, who made motion to reach out and touch someone with her 1911.

"No, you don't!" Hawthorne yelped. She leapt off the runners and stomped a heavy boot on the culprit's wrist. The gun skittered from Love's hand.

"She doesn't have a very strong grip, does she?" Davecki said.

"An old war wound," Angel Kelly said.

"War wound?"

Kelly stared at Davecki with knowledge in her eyes.

"Oh man. Seriously?"

"Yup. Iraq. And, get this, she was a warrant officer."

"Incredible. Father and daughter both flew helicopters?"

"Yup," Kelly said. "Time's wasting, Dave. What's it gonna be? Stay or go back?"

Davecki looked down.

Stanski did what most basket riders do, tipped the sled over and fell face first in the snow. Sputtering, he barrel rolled over to Love's weapon. Picked it up. "You won't be needing this where you're going, *ma'am.*"

"I told you not to call me that," Kitty Love hissed.

"Oh, I forgot, *ma'am.* I won't call you *ma'am* ever again, *ma'am.*"

"Anyone ever tell you you're a real jerk?" Love asked.

"I get that a lot, *ma'am,*" Stanski said, getting to his feet.

While law enforcement did their duty, dog enforcement did theirs. Rampart and Rembrandt licked Davecki's face. Regal sniffed and nose-nudged Daniel Day-Lewis. Ranger whined and rubbed eyes and nose on Davecki's arm. Rivka and Raymond put four forepaws on Davecki's chest in the doggy version of CPR. The rest of the R-dogs sniffed and snuffed around Davecki wondering if Silly Hooman was alive or dead.

Above, Davecki said, "Isn't that precious."

"True," Kelly said. "Dogs are the best of the best of the best."

Back at law enforcement, Stanski cuffed Love to the sled.

Hawthorne rushed to Davecki. Shoving dogs aside, she cried, "Dave! Honey! You okay?"

Davecki glanced at Kelly. "You hear that? She called me honey!"

Kelly grinned and nodded.

Going to her knees in the pool of man's best friends gathered around Davecki, Hawthorne cradled his face and kissed him on the lips. "Don't leave me, Dave!" she commanded.

"Holy Mackerel," Davecki said. "Did you hear that, Kelly? She called me honey and kissed me! I'm outta here!"

As Davecki dove for the world below, Kelly yelled, "Just remember I helped stop that bullet!"

The first things Davecki saw upon opening his weary blue eyes were Hawthorne's stunning green eyes. "I love you, Brekken," he said.

"Atta boy, Davie," Hawthorne said. "I always knew there was a crack in your armor somewhere."

Meanwhile back at the dog sled, Stanski said, "Love! Stay!"

"You like an ignoramus or something?" Kitty Love asked, staring at the deputy. "I'm going to jump up and run away while handcuffed to a dog sled?"

"There's that," Stanski said with a grin. He ran to the budding romance. "If you two lovebirds will excuse me, I'll take this sled up to Pratt's Peak for a cell signal and call for the helicopter."

"I'm okay! I'm okay," Davecki said. "Don't." Besides, he thought, Crazy Love might somehow steal it and get away.

With feeble moves he shrugged out of Hawthorne's embrace, pushed furry friends around and settled on the Polaris seat. "This thing is too noisy," he said, shutting off the idling snowmobile. "She shot me in the back!"

"I was wondering what kind of excuse you had for laying around like a slacker," Stanski said.

"Let's get a look," Hawthorne said.

She helped Davecki unzip his Carhartt and struggle out of the sleeves. The Clavicle Brothers cracked yet again. Davecki thought, that won't be happening when I get to heaven for real. On the outside he said, "Owie, owie, owie!"

"Suck it up, buttercup," Stanski said.

"Easy for you to say," Hawthorne said. She pulled the Carhartt away, handed it to Stanski.

Stanski stuck his finger through the bullet hole in the jacket back. "Will you look at that," he said.

"Amazing," Hawthorne said.

They looked at each other, grinning.

"Knock it off you two! Tell me how bad it is!"

Rampart kissed Davecki's face.

"Phew! Your breath stinks, Dog." On the inside he thought, Brekken's kiss was way nicer.

"Somebody tell me. I can take it."

"You do it," Hawthorne said.

"No. By all means. I always defer to love interest," Stanski said.

"Knock it off, you two!" Davecki yelled.

"Settle down, honey," Hawthorne said. She patted his shoulder. "You're going to be fine. The bullet hit one of the rivets in your Carhartts and shattered."

Honey, Davecki thought. I could get used to her calling me honey.

"A mere flesh wound, buddy," Stanski said.

I like that too, Davecki thought. "Good to hear," he said.

"Hey! Love triangle! Would someone mind officially arresting me? All the mushy stuff is making me sick to my stomach," Love yelled.

"Oh, pardon me," Stanski said. "Apparently Love can't wait. This is your collar, Brekken."

"No. You take it," Hawthorne said.

"You could do rock, paper, scissors," Davecki volunteered.

"Oh, for crying out loud! Would one of you jackasses decide?" Love said.

"Did she say please?" Stanski asked.

"Oh, my God," Love muttered.

"I think you better say please," Davecki advised. "Or they'll be debating the collar all night."

"Up yours," Love said.

"Criminals these days. They're so impolite," Hawthorne said.

"True," Stanski said. "Still. I think you should arrest her. It'll look good on your service record. Big time arrest of a veterinarian handcuffed to a dog sled."

"Alright already...*PLEASE*?" Love said.

"She's asking nice," Davecki said. "Someone should decide."

Hawthorne glanced around. "Is this Reservation land?"

Stanski studied the trees. "Hard to say. What do you think, Dave?"

Davecki said, "Well, at some point all the trees look alike in the night. If I had to guess, I'd say, probably not."

"Huh," the trio said in unison as they looked at the surrounding forest for the trees.

"Lord, help me," Love prayed.

Hey Kelly, Davecki thought/prayed, Love needs some love. You available?

"Finally, Love wants to know what love is," Kelly whispered in Davecki's ear. *"We're on it."*

Sounds reasonable, Davecki thought. Snapping back to reality, he said, "I'm pretty sure we're too far away to be on the Rez."

"Then, by all means," Hawthorne gestured Stanski toward Love.

"Thank God," Love said.

"Like I said," Kelly whispered again.

Stanski walked over to Love, said, "Well then, ma'am, you are under arrest. You have the right to remain silent...."

"Don't call me ma'am," Love said.

Stanski read Love her rights.

Hawthorne helped Davecki back into his Carhartt. They sat on the Polaris seat. He lowered his weary head, resting it on Hawthorne's strong steady shoulder.

In this case, the wheels of justice didn't take forever to return the Rolex to the rightful heir. Kaylee sold it and used the proceeds to run her first Iditarod, winning both the Red Lantern and the Leonhard Seppala awards. She promptly enrolled in vet school.

Sponsors:

Gold Level

Redpaw.

ironriverpizzaparlor.com 715-372-4005

HOLLA HOLLA! FOR THE Pizza Parlor

68285 SOUTH MAIN STREET IRON RIVER WISCONSIN

Silver Level

carhartt.

Norvado

Platinum Level

MIDLAND Energy

Welcome to Brule

CENEX®

Order additional copies of

Gold, Greed, and Good Dogs

at

www.savpress.com

Trace Davecki's career in these volumes